PENGUIN MO?

Mall(

JIBANANANDA DAS was born in Barisal, East Bengal (British India), in 1899 in a Brahmo family. He spent most of his adult life traveling from Barisal to Calcutta and back again—frequently unemployed and destitute, working intermittently as an English professor at various colleges and briefly as a life insurance agent, and writing poetry, an activity that did not always go over well with his employers. Jibanananda's poetry was enthusiastically taken up by the *adhunik* (modernist) poets of the post-Tagore generation associated with little magazines such as *Kallol*, *Pragati*, *Kavita* and others, although Jibanananda remained somewhat tangential to the group. After the Partition of 1947, Jibanananda moved to Calcutta and died there in a tram accident in 1954. As often happens, his poetry found a much greater following in both Bengals after his death, and he remains one of the most celebrated poets in the Bangla language.

REBECCA WHITTINGTON is a scholar and translator of modern South Asian literatures (Bangla, Tamil, and Hindi-Urdu). She translated poetry and fiction for the anthology *Time Will Write a Song For You: Contemporary Tamil Writing from Sri Lanka* (Penguin India, 2014). She lives in San Francisco with her family, spends time in Kolkata often, and shares Jibanananda's liking for languages, birds, and cats.

JIBANANANDA DAS

Malloban

Translated from the Bengali by Rebecca Whittington

PENGUIN BOOKS

An imprint of Penguin Random House

PENGUIN BOOKS

USA | Canada | UK | Ireland | Australia
New Zealand | India | South Africa | China

Penguin Books is part of the Penguin Random House group of companies
whose addresses can be found at global.penguinrandomhouse.com

Published by Penguin Random House India Pvt. Ltd
4th Floor, Capital Tower 1, MG Road,
Gurugram 122 002, Haryana, India

First published in Penguin Books by Penguin Random House India 2022

English translation and introduction copyright © Rebecca Whittington 2022

ISBN 9780143451686

Typeset in Bembo Std by Manipal Technologies Limited, Manipal

www.penguin.co.in

Translator's Dedication

To my mother . . .

CONTENTS

INTRODUCTION

For many readers in India, Bangladesh, and beyond, Jibanananda Das is a name synonymous with "poet." Jibanananda's* impressive body of prose work, which includes short stories and novels, was unearthed from a chest years after his death—perhaps not surprising for the poet of *Dhusar Pandulipi* (Gray Manuscripts). These experimental works were unquestionably ahead of their time, and, arguably, there is still nothing quite like them in the world of Bangla fiction. This makes the prose-writer Jibanananda something of a writer's writer, in contrast to the much-beloved poet-Jibanananda; however, since the publication of a substantial number of the prose works, along with previously unpublished poems, in the twelve-volume *Jibanananda Samagra* (Complete Jibanananda, ed. Debesh Ray) in the 1980s–1990s, Jibanananda's fiction has gained a cult following. To my knowledge, only a fraction of Jibanananda's prose has been published in English translation.

Malloban is the third of four novels Jibanananda wrote in Calcutta in 1948, just after the Partition. *Malloban* takes

---

* The Bangla convention is to refer to authors by their given names.

us back to the winter of 1929 in Calcutta, in the wake of
the Swadeshi movement that arose after the first Partition of
Bengal in 1905 and at the beginning of the global economic
depression. The three subsequent novels take place closer
to the time of writing: *Basmatir Upakhyan* in East Bengal on
the eve of Partition, *Jalpaihati* in East Bengal and Calcutta
around the Partition, and *Sutirtha* in post-Partition Calcutta.
This quartet, though clearly shaped by the upheavals of
the 1940s, decenters the traumatic events of the period to
dwell on the slower processes of wear and tear in the fabric
of everyday life, the dysfunctionality of language, and the
limits of empathy.

Lyrical, grotesque, and deadpan by turns, *Malloban*
portrays with devastating perception the damaging effects
of rigid norms of gender and sexuality along with the loss
of human connection with fellow humans, and with nature,
that comes out of the combined forces of colonialism,
capitalism, and urbanization. The main characters are a small
family living in North Calcutta's College Street, an area also
known as boipara (book neighborhood) for its publishing
houses and bookstalls. For the protagonist Malloban, an office
clerk employed by a foreign company, the neighborhood's
main attraction is the Goldighi (literally "Round Pond,"
a reservoir in what is now known as Vidyasagar Square).
Malloban, his wife Utpala, and their eight-year-old daughter
Monu go about their daily life neatly separated from their
neighbors by a "splendid partition" of green tarpaulins.
Meanwhile, Malloban accommodates the widening gulfs
within their small family with an increasingly painful and
feverish awareness of his isolation in a "sea of individuals,"
framed at various points in the novel by invocations and

inversions of contemporary (late-colonial) discourses of class, caste, race, and gender. Particularly arresting are moments when a sudden gap appears in the dense weave of Malloban's interior discourse, letting Utpala's or even more rarely, Monu's thoughts show through briefly.

The mundane and circular narrative of the deterioration of this small, ordinary family (self-designated as lower middle class), structured as a series of vignettes of everyday dysfunction and discontent, is underpinned by a sense of human alienation from the natural world as a series of real and symbolic encounters with urban and proverbial wildlife build up to a crisis of belief in the possibility of compassion. At least thirty different species of birds feature in the novel, from common city birds like the house crow to jungle birds like the hornbill and exotic residents of the Alipur zoo like the macaw. The shamkol or Asian openbill stork, various other members of the stork, heron, and crane families, and the hornbill, known in Bangla as dhanesh or "the lord of wealth," play a central role opposite parakeets and peafowls, acquiring cumulative and changing meanings as symbols of Malloban and Utpala's desires; in one striking scene, they see each other's failings in the strutting of a pigeon; and even when Malloban seems to have lost all faith in the human capacity for empathy, he senses a deep compassion on the part of the ordinary house crow. Similarly, at least twenty-five different species of trees and plants (both gach in Bangla) find a place in the novel's ecosystem, though mostly in memories of Malloban's home village. Interestingly, mammals, our closest relatives in the animal world, evoke much greater ambivalence, embodying the grotesque, violent, pestilential, or pathetic—in short, too close for comfort. Meanwhile, Malloban's self-perception as a long-suffering person finds concrete expression in his tolerance of parasitic insects. From this description, the presence of diverse flora and fauna in the novel may appear purely symbolic of the characters' mental states; however, such a reading would miss the fundamental obsession of this and many of Jibanananda's writings with uncomfortable coexistence, with the need to suffer each other, and feel each other's suffering against the grain of our increasing distance from any natural balance. The self-absorbed yet ruthless honesty of this portrayal is in sharp contrast to a novel like Bibhutibhushan Bandyopadhyay's *Aranyak* (Of the Forest, written in 1937–39), where the bhadralok protagonist's guilt about the environmental destruction of which he is an instrument as an estate manager is ultimately rendered as something sad and noble, along with a strong dose of exoticism. *Malloban* can, thus, be read as, yet is irreducible to, a portrait of late-colonial Calcutta, of middle-class life, or of domestic discord; its ecological perspective makes it extremely timely in the present moment.

The critical presence of (nonhuman) animals in the novel throws the human constructions of class, caste, gender, and sexuality into relief as human violence is unfavorably compared to the violence of nature. This adds a unique dimension to the novel's portrayal of the middle-class/upper-caste bhadralok, who were the most commonly represented in modern and modernist Bangla fiction, though there were several notable novels about working communities written by bhadralok authors—for example, Manik Bandyopadhyay's *Padma Nadir Majhi* (Boatman of the River Padma, 1936), Tarashankar Bandyopadhyay's

Hansuli Banker Upakatha (The Tale of Hansuli Turn, 1951),
Satinath Bhaduri's *Dhorai Charit Manas* (1949 and 1951)—
as well as at least one by an author of the Malo community
considered an important forerunner of the Dalit literature
movement (Advaita Mallabarman's *Titash Ekti Nadir
Naam*—Titash Is the Name of a River, completed in 1950
and published posthumously in 1956), which remain classics
of the period. Malloban designates himself as lower middle
class, and his conflicts with Utpala often revolve around
petty sums of money (the price of a second-class movie
ticket, a cup of tea, a gift sari) but are framed by ideas of
gendered behavior which they each see as a root cause of
their sexual frustration and lack of self-fulfillment. Utpala
vents her anger at the Hindu beliefs that "force" her to
accept unhappiness as natural—a statement of protest that
Malloban finds perfectly scientific, even if he concludes in
the end that her feelings are "beyond science." Meanwhile,
from their unspecified position somewhere on the privileged
end of the caste spectrum (notably, they are not Brahmos
but Hindus), they recognize the speciousness of caste logic
even as they demonstrate their own complicity with caste
prejudice and violence as well as colorism. For example, in
an exchange about their domestic help, Malloban is struck
by the absurdity of Utpala's comment: "All kinds of scandals
go on among the lower castes." "Lower castes? Bhadurani's
a Brahmin's daughter." "That may be. Fine then . . . Thakur
is a Brahmin too . . ." yet he is equally guilty of perpetuating
deeply problematic associations between caste, character,
female beauty, and skin color and of using the names of
human communities as insults without a second thought. As
Malloban's personal crisis mounts, these moments lay bare

the limits of Malloban's compassion—he is pained by the sexual vulnerability of a woman who works at his boarding house, for example, but she appears as a grotesque figure with nonhuman features—echoing his perception of Utpala in a rapid series of animal forms—and he withdraws from the scene without comment. By contrast, the sufferings of a kitten and a goat send him into deep philosophical reflection on the violence of humankind, inducing a short-lived vegetarianism. This makes it possible to read the novel as a critique of the discourse of ahimsa, and specifically its failure to fundamentally change perceptions about marginalized communities.

Malloban's intense and multifaceted engagement with language as not only a medium of artistic expression, but as its subject—language as a lost landscape, a flock of thought-birds, a nest on a winter's night, a weapon of bitterness, a beautiful, superfluous body we sculpt and adorn, adore, and lament—is more than enough to earn it a place as a modern classic of world literature. The Bangla modernism of Jibanananda and his contemporaries was in conversation with Euro-American modernism, a conversation structured unequally by orientalism; but each germinated and grew in its own way, as a part of its own ecosystem. No further argument needs to be made here. In India and South Asia, since Jibanananda's prose has not been widely translated into English or into other languages of the subcontinent, and conversely, he did not read any other languages himself besides Bangla and English, the importance of this novel does not lie so much in a direct exchange of artistic ideas, unlike other Bengali novelists before and after him whose work was and is well known in other regions. However, readers of Jibanananda's poetry will find that reading the prose adds many layers of depth and complexity to understanding his work as a whole. Jibanananda's prose is darkly funny and suffused with his inimitable poetic sensibility, marked by characteristic shifts between formal, colloquial, and dialectal Bangla and manipulation of idiomatic language, as discussed at length in the note on the translation below. Finally, it is simply a striking work of literature in a regional language, and it is an honor to share it with readers beyond Bengal.

NOTE ON THE TITLE AND
CHARACTER NAMES

As all Jibanananda's prose works were published after his death, many were given titles by the editors; however, Malloban is the author's own title. Malloban literally means "the one wearing a garland," suggesting the exchange of garlands in a Hindu wedding ceremony; in mythology, exchanging of garlands itself constitutes a gandharva wedding—the short and sweet version for ancient "love marriages." While this name would conventionally be transliterated as Malyaban, I chose to represent it more phonetically to approximate the Bangla pronunciation, even if this makes it less likely that the reader will recognize the ironic reference. The name also refers to a mythical mountain, associatively linked in the text with the Sahyadri or "Mountains of Patience," the northern part of the Western Ghats mountain range. The name Utpala means a lotus or water lily, while Monu is a common daknaam or nickname, perhaps from mon (heart/mind), though many daknaam are simply sounds without any literal meaning.

NOTE ON THE TRANSLATION

This novel adopted me for its own mysterious reasons, like a cat, and I haven't been able to get rid of it since. Knowing that translating Jibanananda is an impossible task, I began working on it in 2009, completed the first draft in 2011, wrote an MA thesis on it in 2013, revised the translation in fits and starts over the years, couldn't resist digressing to write a little more about it in my doctoral dissertation in 2019, began to look at it from a new perspective as my research drew me towards Dalit, Adivasi, and women's literary self-representation, and finally thought seriously about publishing it in 2020 while bird-watching from a Kolkata veranda and on walks around the Lake (Rabindra Sarobar).

It is a laughable understatement to say that *Malloban* was not easy to translate. The novel's Bangla shifts frequently between registers, estranging idiomatic expressions, and unsettling received linguistic categories. At first glance, the language of both narration and dialogue in the novel is chalit bhasha or "current language." This language variety, close to the spoken language of Kolkata and neighboring areas and emulated throughout Bengal by people with the

privilege of higher education, gradually became accepted
as the literary standard over the course of the modernist
period to which Jibanananda's work belongs, replacing
the sadhu bhasha or "refined language" developed during
the nineteenth century. For reference, we can bookend
Malloban (1948) with Manik Bandyopadhyay's *Padma
Nadir Majhi*, written in sadhu bhasha, and Tarashankar
Bandyopadhyay's *Hansuli Banker Upakatha* in chalit bhasha
or Advaita Mallabarman's *Titash Ekti Nadir Naam* in sadhu
bhasha; the choice of sadhu or chalit at the time did not
follow a linear trajectory, and the above texts also made
extensive use of socio-regional dialects. An updated form
of chalit bhasha remains standard today in Bangla literature
from both West Bengal and Bangladesh. The chalit
bhasha of *Malloban*, however, seems bent on exposing its
own contradictions—Malloban's interior discourse spills
over into the dialogue, where his own half-literary, half-
colloquial language and the violent excess of Utpala's highly
idiomatic language play out their irreconcilable desires
through familiar and peculiar figurations. This produces a
physical sensation of linguistic incongruence. His language
is not mukher bhasha, "of the mouth," nor is it the divinely
sweet language of bodily fluids, nor is it "literary." What is
"literary"? Malloban seems to think of his own thoughts as
drafts of literary compositions, full of awkward figures and
crossings-out, even as they follow his body's tossing and
turning in bed and circling in the city streets. At the same
time, this awkwardness points to Malloban's uprootedness,
his drifting between nostalgia for a village 150 miles away
and multifarious reflections on the daily grind in Kolkata
and the fate of Bengalis, while Utpala's command over

Kolkata idiom corresponds to her determination to make a place for herself in the city.

This heightened awareness of language as a work in progress—and sometimes as an utter failure, depending on what we expect it to do—prompted me to refrain from imposing any single variety of English on the text. My native language is American English (specifically the English of Northern California and even more specifically the San Francisco Bay Area), my home language is our family variety of Banglish (not a mix of two self-contained languages but a coexistence of multiple dialects of each), and Bangla is an inextricable part of my soundscape; so while remaining conscious of my positioning and of the fact that the book will be published in India, from my personal perspective the language of this translation is neither "domesticated" nor "foreignized," but intuitive and fluid. However, it will inevitably read differently for different readers, sometimes familiar and sometimes strange. I hope each reader enjoys this in their own way. I have avoided egregious Americanisms in the translation, but I have made no attempt to reproduce the English of a Bangla speaker/ writer in the 1920s or to imitate South Asian English usage, though I have consistently retained any English words found in the novel, as well as words borrowed from other languages—for example, "lorry" and "Nippon." This decision comes from my sense that although *Malloban* is set in a specific time and place, it is not a period piece in terms of its language. The novel's insistence on disrupting "naturalness" defies the project of reproduction in favor of refraction, its language, obscure and lucid by turns, splits and bends at varied angles the gendered ideologies of domesticity, women's rights, nationalism, capitalism, etc., of the novel's time of writing and setting. In another sense, the novel's language is a play of resonances and dissonances reverberating within and between bodies. For these reasons, I have followed my instincts and allowed the language of the translation to be multiple.

On the other hand, my translation tends strongly towards the literal in terms of vocabulary and syntax, sometimes at the risk of pushing the boundaries of comprehension. This stems from Jibanananda's idiosyncratic sentence structure, punctuation, and compound words, and from the relationship of these stylistic features to the construction of space, place, and displacement. A passage may open matter-of-factly and seem to demand a straightforward colloquial rhythm or even a terse choppiness, then begin to flow and reach lyrical heights until interrupted by a knot of impossibly awkward yet strangely compelling words or phrases. This is evident in the opening pages of the novel, which map out Malloban's habitations and preoccupations. While some punctuation that differs from English is conventional in Bangla, such as the use of dashes for lines of dialogue instead of quotation marks, Jibanananda has a strong penchant for dashes and semicolons, sometimes in unexpected places, and for omitting commas where they might be expected, creating a proliferation of gaps and abrupt pauses alternating with poetic cadences, so I have mostly retained the punctuation as is. The most challenging aspect of the text for translation is its heavy and often unconventional use of idioms, forcing me to walk a fine line between domestication and exoticism. Although this is true of any translation to some extent, the violence channeled through this novel's idiomatic language is impossible to ignore—the violence of convention on the one hand, and the violence of being torn out of context on the other. I have, therefore, not been able to avoid this violence in the translation either, at the risk of adding an extra layer of oddness to the language. I think that this risk is balanced by the need to resist the smoothed-out, "reads-like-it-was-written-in-English" model of translation, and that a compelling literary work pulls the reader into its world, however close or distant that world may be geographically, culturally, or linguistically. Except in places where there is an English idiom that is semantically almost identical or felicitously captures a different aspect of the passage, I have chosen to trust the reader to put some effort into figuring out the delicate web of relations that a collocation holds together.

For similar reasons, I have retained many Bangla words on a case-by-case basis, including many that will be thoroughly familiar to the non-Bengali South Asian reader, such as "saheb," and some that will not, such as shamkol, a variant spelling of shamuk-khol, "snail-shell," or more interpretively "snail opener," the Asian openbill stork (Anastomus oscitans). It was often difficult to choose between the evocative Bangla common names of flora and fauna, which have associative or symbolic meanings in the text, and the English common names which would give the nature-loving reader a visual image of the species, so I have used the Bangla names most concentrated with contextual significance and the English names when they appear in a list form or litany.

In sum, I have done this translation "on the authority of my own mind," as the protagonist of *Karubashona* puts it, while "feeling [my] shortcomings in every bone," as Malloban does. Any errors are entirely mine. I hope that you will find "many important and unanticipated things" in it.

MALLOBAN

ONE

All that day Malloban hadn't even thought of it; but at night, lying in bed, among many other things he remembered that forty-two years ago he had been born on exactly this day—today is the twentieth of Aghran.

So forty-two years of his life have gone by.

It's almost one in the morning. In the city of Kolkata, it's quite cold; he's finished dinner and climbed under the covers around ten o'clock or so; sleep should have come to him by now, but it hasn't; sometimes sleep just won't come. It's right on College Street, Malloban's little two-story rented house; the house is not bad by the look of it—but it's not very big—still, it's not too cramped. There are four rooms upstairs—three of them rented out to another family—they've screened off a separate block for themselves—they seem self-contained and self-contented—they don't make much of an effort to be neighborly.

The remaining room on the second floor belongs to Malloban and his family; his wife Utpala has arranged the room so beautifully it's a pleasure to see. A few pictures are hung on the bright white walls; a bromide enlargement; of a middle-aged man, her father perhaps, an oil-painting of her mother; photographs of a few more of Malloban's in-laws—a few sketches (who drew them?)—inside the room a polished mahogany bedstead, a bedcover white as an egret's wing always spread over the thick mattress and topper. Two human beings sleep in this bed; Utpala ("Pala" to people her own age, her elders, almost everybody) and her daughter Monu. The daughter is around nine years old. In these twelve years of Malloban and Utpala's married life, only this one girl has come along. And there will be nothing more, that's settled. This second-floor room is quite big, the floor always neat and clean, never a piece of paper, ribbon, safety-pin, or speck of powder lying around; inside the room there are a few pieces of furniture, table, chair, sofa, couch; not everything is in perfect condition, some things are torn, stained, but thanks to Utpala's efforts, nothing shows. In one corner there's an organ, next to it a sitar and an esraj; the things that light up Utpala's life; she loves to sing, likes to play instruments too, in the midst of all her activities she's almost always humming her way around some tune or other, sometimes even a kirtan; sometimes, especially in the bathroom under running water, Pala sings out nice and loud. Malloban knows nothing about singing, but he's made a habit of putting up with his wife's vocalizations, her sharajrishabhgandhar or whatever, very patiently; otherwise, Dushto Saraswati would start her mischief, and then there would be no saving him. But still, he finds it very tedious, not just his wife's singing, he feels so disillusioned with all the world's music, he can't even think what to do about it. Utpala's face would go white as lime, her ears would start ringing, her eyes would burn, if he told her to stop, to stop singing. He has never managed to mold himself into the proper object of his wife's affections and esteem. Malloban thinks of himself as a crackling alum; he keeps to himself; he's in the habit of forgiving people, doesn't like to taint himself with uncalled-for hoo-ha and spite. He's a peace-loving man; even at the expense of his own comfort and convenience. He never says much to his wife about her singing; although if he feels extremely afflicted, he makes his grievance known with a few significant statements such as "Singing takes serious training," "A lot of people sing wholeheartedly, and it's good, it's good because they do it wholeheartedly—" This kind of hint gets him serious punishment from his wife; so, if possible, he refrains entirely from comment.

It's not that Malloban doesn't like song and dance himself. Before he got tied down to his Kolkata job, when he was out in the country, in his childhood, at the end of some winter nights he loved to hear the baul songs; all those melodies would come floating through the darkness from above some far-off hijol forest and give his youthful guts a wrench. So many days—when the day came to a close—on his way home after a game of bat and ball, over the ridge paths between the fields of new autumn paddy, kalijira, dhanshali, rupshali, his heart would stir at the sound of the bhatiali songs; all the words and deeds of all the day would sink down like an exhausted flounder into some abysmal tank, and the water above would strike up a glittering pitter patter of drops—the songlike water, the waterlike song, all around the shade of the khejurchari, rippling coconuts, rustling tamarisks, darkness inside a star; he would sit quiet on one edge of things. So many nights he's slipped out of the house and gone to hear the jatra—and afterwards those

songs would take such hold of him that, time and again, in
the middle of memorizing for a test, he would have to rest
his head on the table and keep still for a long time. Like
the sky of the month of Boishakh, empty of clouds and full
of the sparkling of fireflies, his mind would brim edge to
edge; like a foreboding that he might thrust his face into the
pillow and start to sob; but just in time he would straighten
up his head and try to direct himself into another world,
he wouldn't sob. There was a gentleman by the name
of Manibhupkantha Chakrabarti—was his name really
Manibhupkantha? What does that name even mean? And
yet everyone called him by that name . . . He remembered
Manibhup singing; and Shamanhara Bose—Jhunu—better
known by the name of Jhunu Bose-Chaudhurani; where
have those days gone? As soon as he sat down at the edge of
a gathering, tempted away from his studies by performances
here and there across town, his uncle would show up and
drag him home by the ear—and still he wouldn't hesitate to
make an accomplice of his mother and run off again.

   Malloban has told none of this to Pala.

   In the upstairs room, Pala (Utpala) and Monu sleep.
In the downstairs room is Malloban's bed, his parlor—
everything. Here he lives, speaks, works, reads, writes,
reclines, sleeps. He has not become detached from his wife
like this of his own accord. That one room upstairs just
isn't room enough for Utpala, so she's told her husband
to make his own sleeping arrangements in the downstairs
room. And yet the upstairs room is much bigger than the
downstairs room—light and air, sunshine, all the edges of
blue sky, and the big blueness of the sky itself quite face-
to-face with nature, with humanity; the first floor looks out

on the astonishing expanse of a huge terrace, but if you go up just two steps of the staircase, the whole terrace of the first floor, the sky, the sunshine, the city of Kolkata itself is yours; if you can only imagine it, the whole history of the world's cities and citizens, of Babylon itself, will bubble up before your eyes.

Two creatures—isolated in these two rooms, above and below. Malloban got married almost twelve years ago. For two or three years after the marriage, Pala went back and forth, staying mainly in her father's house; after that she stayed a few years in her in-laws' house, Monu came along, and when Monu was just six months old she went back to her father's house; she spent another two years there, until her father's death, and for these past seven years or so she's been with her husband in Kolkata.

One in the morning. Malloban turned over on his right side and tried to sleep a little; various things creep into his mind—sleep keeps slipping away. Then, slowly turning over on his left side, he thought how nice it would be to sleep now. But the clock's struck one-thirty, then two, and sleep has not come; some nights are like this.

Pulling the blanket up to his lips and closing his eyes, he turned over once more. All sorts of sounds fall into his ears from the streets of Kolkata. It's two in the morning, after all, and the cold is cruel, but still someone's carriage seems to be clattering over the street; inside the car, the laughter of girls, the thick voices of old men, the clamor of children. Malloban, lying fishlike beneath the blanket, was thinking: really, where are you going, you clerks, where are you coming back from? While the sound of horses' hooves could still be heard clearly at a distance, the monstrous jolt of an engine suddenly swallowed up all the surrounding sounds. A lorry came and went. It seemed to Malloban that even this moribund lorry-voice has some significance—as if oil could be extracted from sand; if he didn't assume this to be the sound of wheels or tires and took it instead for the torrential voice of a clouded night, then how lovely the lorry's— A bit of plaster came off the ceiling and fell onto Malloban's nose and mouth; the lorry sped off, shaking the house's foundations, baap re, just like the tidal wave of Nippon, thought Malloban, brushing the whitewash off of his nose and mouth. Some Kahar-Mahato people are carrying a corpse down the road. It sounds like somebody's private car has come to a halt right by Malloban's house— as if the car has broken down somehow; a few mechanics are trying to repair it; the smell of Mobil Oil crept into Malloban's nose, he found it not unpleasant; a bull going along the footpath snorted once; right out front, as if from someone's second floor, a voluminous, indistinct sound of crying and arguing can be heard; right by Malloban's room, near the drain, a mangy dog has been rooting around in the rubbish for a long time, pawing and clawing, as if playing on a sandglass—what does he want? What will he find? At a little distance, in the interior of a house—maybe in a basement, in a storeroom, in a warehouse, two cats have been fighting in deadly earnest for some time; one of them is male and the other female, no doubt; on this winter night, in this astonishing cold, under pretense of a fight, this passing-strange outburst of blood and lust, this deadly mischief of cats in heat—Malloban was thinking, with parted teeth—cats do brawl and scuffle and yowl; Malloban had seen an old white-bearded professor, married late in life, doing just the same around seven years ago—in the evening; Malloban had entered this professor's room in rubber-soled shoes, without clearing his throat; of course he'd never suspected that this sort of scandalous business might be going on; but from that very moment, Malloban has begun to appreciate the fact that humans have become themselves precisely by breaking and scattering, burning and stirring up the strange heat, passion, and thorough-going baseness of the great synthesis at which one arrives after analyzing all baser life forms. Malloban wore himself out thinking and turned over again. The clock struck two-thirty, but sleep did not come.

Today was his birthday. Forty-two years ago today—on the twentieth of the month of Aghran, in a village of Bengal almost a hundred and fifty miles from Kolkata—he had been born. There the rows of date palms are more, the palmyra groves are less, and the scent of betel may be more than anything. In cold weather just like this, a pipe is driven into the heads of the date palms and a pot bound to their necks, and all through the winter night, the sap oozes out drop by drop, flies and bees and tiny nocturnal butterflies, big ones too, swim in that pot of sap, wave their wings, lie dead; all this can be seen in the cold-dense fog-desolate night's end. On a winter night like this, the rice fields lie empty—the whole field is covered in yellow stubble; feeling the cold, a couple of tigers come down; on a sad night just like this, the jackals at least laugh uproariously; in the cremation ground, the pallbearers' chants of "Hari bol" sound like the muffled cries of far-off fog-men; the barn owls hoot incessantly; if his sleep breaks and he goes and stands outside, he can see, through the gaps of the last wrench of winter fog, the stars—Brihaspati, Kalpurush, Abhijit, Sirius—as if going back and forth on some distant path, lantern in hand and accompanied by a marvelous, far-off, otherworldly jingling. Some days there's less fog—there are white clouds—alongside an unfurling strip of cloud—the moon at a standstill with its own vast body of light. Until the age of twenty-five or twenty-seven, he often went back to the country, he was there to see and hear these things, but fifteen years have gone by since then, this city has become his only home, the thought of glass-beetles and honeybees, of shamkol storks and mouchushki sunbirds, of fireflies, doesn't even cross his mind, he doesn't even turn to look at the constellations in the sky.

Carried away by his thoughts, he forgot all about those silvery-greenish fire-clusters in the sky. Last month, after fifteen years at one job, he got a raise to two hundred and fifty rupees a month; before that, his salary was one hundred ninety-five; for nearly five years it was just one hundred ninety-five rupees; before that it had fluctuated. Malloban worked for sahebs, true enough, but the office used to be in such bad shape that he had to endure for too many years the discomforts of living on his nominal starting salary. Some of the other clerks left the office then, but Malloban didn't go anywhere; instead, he kept slogging away in this same office. Tonight, he feels he has gotten his reward for so many days of service.

Service? What more can he say? With the meager strength and opportunity his forefathers have given him, there's no way he could have dedicated himself to the country, to mankind, to the law, to medicine, even to education. If he had gone down any of those paths, no one would have respected him—would they? Even if a man sets his sights high, who will respect him if he stumbles and starts limping? So, for these fifteen years, he's sat and slogged at his own pace for the office of Bottomley Bigland Brothers. What more can he do, will he do?

He had passed his BA and was studying law, but then he got this office job; he took it.

Of course, now and then his mind jumps like a jhumur dancer—if he had become a lawyer, maybe it wouldn't have been a bad life, he could have lived quite independently, he wouldn't have had to compete with anyone, if he managed to advance in the business, there would be plenty of prestige to be gained. There are times when he thinks these things. But when he takes a good look at the bar libraries of the outstations . . . sees and hears how the big M.L.s and D.L.s of Kolkata are losing out everywhere to the district-committee-passed P.L.s in the business of earning a living— he sometimes laughs to himself—not out of smugness, not out of complacency, but feeling his own shortcomings in every bone. Malloban has realized that he would never have been able to do anything better than the work he is doing. Maybe he would have been a minor inspector or superintendent, and it isn't even that he couldn't have gone all the way to the highest commissioner's post, if he'd fallen into the government service track; from the financial perspective, he certainly would have made some profit, and he wants money, wants it badly, but he'd wanted many other things too—knowledge more than anything. He wanted to go very far in his studies, longed to learn many things, to understand them—longed to make it understood to people that his own mind is not at all a clerkish, desk-

pinned, toilsome, insipid thing. Various longings—he longs
to make it known that his mind produces all sorts of sound,
orderly, structured ideas; there are times when he feels like
leaving his office job and the life he is leading and diving
into the foamy crest of some great work—some exciting
workers' union, for instance; what's the use of beating
down and suffocating life with this kind of office drudgery?
Money—familial prosperity—at times all these things seem
like so many seeds of grass, of sponge-gourd, of cotton.
Strolling around the Goldighi reservoir, stick in hand,
he feels he possesses an extraordinary ability to address a
huge thunderstruck assembly, expressing himself with great
elegance and astonishing restraint in a vast, shoreless sea of
emotion. In politics these days, Bengalis are being turned
back in shame at every step by Gujaratis, Marathis, Madrasis,
UPites—his blood boils just thinking about it, he feels like
rising up all ablaze with an irrepressible fire to reclaim
the honor and dignity of Bengalis—from revolution to
revolution—France, Russia, Spain, China—in the—what
do you call it—in the nipple-peak of all the revolutions, the
exultation of new milk for a new world.

Carried away again, he forgets the Bengalis. A long
while later, his head begins to cool off; then, sitting on a
bench by the Goldighi, he slowly quiets down, lights a
beedi. Feeling hungry, he gets up and starts for home.

One thing is certain: rooting for tubers underground
like a pig, (upper grade) clerkdom is not his all—he doesn't
like to make himself conspicuous, sporting a pair of silk
stockings, varnished New Cut shoes, a tusser coat, neatly
parted hair, a cigarette case, and a bench on the soccer
ground. He's detached from all that.

He reads the newspaper daily, but not with any special preference for sports, races, highway robberies, scandals exposed in some women's quarters, in some court somewhere, what's playing in which cinema—in all these forty-two years, he's never managed to manufacture much taste or enthusiasm for all that. Still, he comes across various necessary and unanticipated things in the paper; returning from the office and lighting a cheroot, he sits there with the newspaper for a long time; one by one, many kinds of desires and resolves play across his mind; then they shatter. After that, he grows dispirited and sets the paper aside; he is left with nothing particular in mind, with a feeling that he has not really learned anything appreciable. Lying in bed, he thinks that surely, he himself will never manage to be a Parnell or Chittaranjan—never—by no procedure—but if no Parnell or Chittaranjan is born among Bengalis these days, then there's very little hope for this race. Malloban lay thinking all this on a night of the year nineteen twenty-nine—that's why his thoughts took this course.

The clock was about to strike three-thirty. Malloban saw that for all this time he's been lying on his back in bed and thinking incessantly, and all that thinking has merely desiccated his heart—there's no shore to be found, not a wink of sleep in his eyes. He sat up slowly. There are bugs in the bed—but it's not the bugs that are keeping him awake, he's spent so many nights of long, uncontested, cunning sleep in the reeking haunts of cockroaches, rats, mosquitoes. The light of a gas lamp in the street was filtering into the room a little; the slippers were sought and found; he slipped them onto his feet, wrapped the red and blue checkered blanket around his whole body, and slowly climbed the stairs to the second floor—edging closer without a sound, he stared fascinated at how unperturbedly Monu and Pala were sleeping inside the mosquito net—how peaceful, how pleased their breathing is. He drew a heavy breath into his core like a lavish kiss and began to let it out slowly, making his whole body delightfully tender—it felt good. It felt good to stare at the sleeping ones—because, on this winter night, Malloban sees fulfilled the main goal of middle-class life—to keep his wife and child in relative prosperity, to provide them with a modicum of comfort, calm, and convenience in their lives. He couldn't sleep himself—what are these two doing in this cold—Sleeping? Waking? That's what he came to see, and he has seen it. Malloban savored the moment—how tender and tangible this night seemed to him, this backwater of the night. Now it's time to go downstairs. Still, he doesn't go just yet. He wants to lift the edge of the mosquito net and duck inside to sit by their bed in affectionate soundlessness, like a quiet-winged bird on a country night in the winter month of Poush—waking them? Or perhaps he won't even sit—he will stroke Monu's brow lightly; the blanket has slipped off his wife's chest, he'll draw it up and tuck it in, lightly. After that he'll go back to his room.

But as soon as he lifted the net, the whole thing went wrong. Utpala woke up in a fright; then she sat up on the bed, and in the upheaval of her whole beautiful face—cutting through that expression in an instant, she said more dryly than the sand of a dead river, "You!"

"I just came."

"Who told you to come at this hour?"

"I came to see what you two were doing."

"Go, take your daughter with you, from tomorrow on she won't sleep with me . . . up against the girl's butt, baap re, like a witch."

"Who, me?" said Malloban, standing there. He didn't sit on the bed, sitting down on a couch, he said, "No, I didn't just come to see the girl, I—"

"Ah, that's it! You sat down! The singer's come to perform at two in the morning. Look at him sitting there, bound hand and foot in the blanket, done up like some kind of sacrificial pumpkin. O ma. O ma—O ma! Get out! Get out, I'm telling you!"

"You were sleeping—I didn't come to disturb your sleep—"

"I'm telling you, sacrificial pumpkin, do you want to be split in two or are you staying here?"

"You were sleeping, sleep."

"You were sleeping sleep! So, guru's pet pumpkin—"

"Why are you going pumpkin-pumpkin, Utpala—"

"It won't do for you to sit here any longer."

"I'm just sitting here for a bit. I won't keep you from sleeping. I'm sitting on this couch, Monu's sleeping, go to sleep."

Utpala cleared her throat—after sleeping six hours at a stretch, her body is deliciously invigorated—and said in a hard voice, dripping with sarcasm, "I've killed all the rats in my room with a leveler, and just in case there's one or two still lurking about I've kept the German traps set out. All that cleverness won't fly. God forbid anything trouble my sleep. If you know what's good for you, you'll go downstairs."

Malloban had been sitting quietly. Not looking and, in any case, not able to see in the dark whether he's gone or still sitting on the couch, Utpala said, "Oh! I wake up and see that rascal standing there by the bed, bundled up in his blanket. All the blood is rushing to my chest and making me dizzy."

"But you saw me standing here."

"If you ever come and scare me like that again—"

"I didn't come to scare you, Ut—"

"No, you've kindly come to show me your beauty. You've come into my room again at this ungodly hour—" Utpala said, gritting her teeth in a strangely all-consuming sense of harassment.

Malloban had been appreciating all the voices of the winter night's soundlessness and lengthiness, that soundless lengthiness, that soundlessness that could have been tenderness (so many times, in the country, it had been so). To alleviate the muggy atmosphere Utpala had created, he said with a short laugh, giving his thin mustache a twist, "If I do come upstairs at an ungodly hour, will you mince me into grasshopper kababs, Pala!" Malloban laughed at his own joke; the laugh stopped short, sensing it had fallen flat; after a little silence, he said finally, "I came tonight—somehow tonight my sleep got spoiled—my sleep got spoiled—I couldn't sleep tonight—"

"Just because you can't sleep yourself, do you have to come and keep other people from sleeping?"

"It's not that."

"Then what is it."

"I came—" Malloban bent his head and calculated for a moment, but failed to come up with anything to say and ended up not saying anything.

Utpala said, "Here you've gone and spoiled my sleep and I'll have to suffer the consequences—I'm not going to be able to get up before eight or nine o'clock."

"That's fine. When you've slept enough, then you'll get up. What more is there to say?"

"My head will be in a vice all day tomorrow."

"When you get up in the morning, drink a cup of hot tea."

"Can you cure a headache just by drinking tea? Idiot!"

"You've got smelling salts and menthol, after all—"

"Can you cure a headache just like that! Huh! Joynath's bullock opened his mouth as he was going around the grinding tree and imparted this wisdom to you, I presume?"

The interior of the mosquito net is nice and warm from Utpala's body—as if they were sleeping inside the warmth of hay, Monu and Pala; if they were not humans but cranes, Malloban was thinking, then he would not still be sitting on the couch but would have snuggled into that nest of theirs ages ago.

"Take a couple of aspirin. But those things aren't so good for you, better not to take them."

"Look, I've caught a chill starting up like that in the middle of the night. I'll have my work cut out for me tomorrow, tearing up rags and twisting them into little wicks and sticking them up my nose and sneezing—it makes me shudder just thinking of it, ugh!"

Malloban got up from the couch, came close to the bed, drew up a lightweight broken-armed chair, and sat down in it quietly.

"We've run out of aspirin, if there was a pill left—"

"You'll have to go buy me a bottle tomorrow."

"I'll do that."

"I'm going to need three or four cups of tea."

"Hot tea does wonders for colds and headaches."

"Yes, it's the cold that brings on this headache."

"Did it just come on?"

"No, it hasn't really come on yet, but it will in the morning, as if Jhagru's wife is beating a hammer on top of the cobbles—that tall dark full-grown woman. Baba re!" Giving herself a backbreaking stretch and letting out a few fitful cries, Utpala said, feeling marvelously rested, "She'll bang that hammer inside my head, that's what. I won't be able to get out of bed. You bring the tea and leave it by my bed, eh, bapu!"

"Is Monu asleep?"

"She's sleeping in her Thakur's shrine."

"What?"

"She's lying there in the Lord's abode, in a trance."

"She's awake?" said Malloban. "Should I call her and see?" But without making any attempt to call Monu, Malloban said, "Tonight I was wide awake all night, didn't get even a wink of sleep. Somehow that's just how it went, not a drop of sleep."

"What time do you have to go to the office tomorrow?"

"Ten thirty."

"I'm going to get up plenty late, maybe eight or nine. Will you be able to make me tea then?"

"Thakur will do it. Or maybe I'll do it."

Wrapping the quilt around her whole body and settling her head on the pillow, Utpala said, "Here, tuck in the mosquito net by Monu's feet, will you."

"There aren't any mosquitoes, it's just a mania of yours to hang the net."

"There aren't any mosquitoes, but there are rats, if I don't tuck in the net, they'll just nibble up our feet."

Fixing the mosquito net, Malloban got up from the chair and went to sit on a dirty, oily sofa. Utpala thrust her head into the pillow, drew up her hands and feet, let out a lazy yawn, rubbed her thumb and finger together, and wrapped the quilt snugly all around her. Then, casting an uncertain glance in Malloban's direction, she said, "You sat down? You sat down, did you?"

"What should I do?"

"Go, go on downstairs."

"What am I going to do there?"

"How long are you going to sit here like this, tell me—"

"I'll just talk with you for a bit—"

"Your tongue will get stuck in your teeth, if you talk too much. You'll get lockjaw. You'll have to prize open your teeth with a spoon—you won't be able to get them open even with a dhenki—go on, scoot—" Utpala turned over.

Malloban stayed sitting there, shivering in the damp and cold, like a wet mop. Nothing to do, nothing to say, he didn't blink, he didn't budge, it seemed unlikely he was even thinking anything.

"What kind of person are you?"

"I'm just sitting here."

"That's what's making me so uncomfortable."

"What am I supposed to do then?"

"Go away."

"Are you going to sleep now?"

"I'll stuff a firebrand in those shameless corpses' faces! Are you going to sleep? Are you going to sleep! At three o'clock in the morning—" Utpala might have burst into tears. But then again, she's no child bride—she's over thirty. Malloban said, letting out a suppressed sigh, "I'm go—ing."

After a little while, Utpala turned to look at him. As if she'd been slapped, she struck back in a taut voice, "You're still sitting there!"

"Look, there's not a wink of sleep in your eyes either anymore."

"It's trapped in your tongue. Get downstairs straightaway. Get—down—"

"I'm going—but the night is almost over anyway."

Utpala sat up on the bed. This time there will be no more talk, it looks like she's spoiling for a fight. But Malloban had retreated inside himself. He had no eyes for what his adversary was doing or not doing. Malloban said, "Yesterday was the twentieth of Aghran. Precisely on this date, the twentieth of Aghran, I was born. Maybe I've told you a few times—do you remember? Since they're your own, things don't stick in your mind. There were so many things to think about on this day—forty-two years of life have gone by. There have been so many crossings of benevolent winds and malevolent winds. Even now there are crossings going on—and they will go on until I rest my head on the earth. And yet—Lalkamal Neelkamal, Red Lotus and Blue Lotus, black winds and white winds, hidden winds of desire and the crone in the moon have conspired to make this life somehow unearthly. I'm an earthly man after all—without earth I'll lose my footing—better a body of gold than of air, better still a body of earth. We're like new grain, in the fragrance of new grain, in a coconut kernel, in the pungency of coconut, in camphor, in jaggery and rice, you and I—that's why I've come to you, why I've sat down here. Give me that. Won't you?"

It's not that Utpala absolutely cannot give him that; she has given it now and then, undoubtedly deep down she's enjoyed it thoroughly, but after a while that attraction has slackened, slackened excessively—though not in equal proportion on both sides. Utpala knows all this. Malloban also knows that nowadays Utpala gets by just fine without certain aspects of conjugal life—clothes and jewelry, food and drink, rest and leisure, pleasure and independence, she doesn't need much else—but it seems Malloban still has need of some aspects in particular, needs them at least a couple days out of many, needs the earthly aspect, not even the golden aspect, needs the earth alone; but for the past five or six years, even if Utpala has sometimes given Malloban a glimpse of her gold, she has maintained no contact with the earth. She's a cloud of the sky—not a blue rain-bearing cloud, but a crackly white cloud, out in the farthest reaches of the sky.

Utpala was lying there with the quilt pulled up to the part in her hair. Her brow is flushed, but she'll have to keep it cool—to sleep. He has babbled on and on before about superior and inferior collectors, servants, demons, Lalkamal Neelkamal—in the midst of all that she has fallen asleep. This kind of thing has happened so many times in her life; after all, today she really must sleep.

"Today is the twentieth of Aghran," said Malloban. "The forefathers and foremothers gave birth to me, after all; life can, after all, be put to plenty of good use; and it has been—hasn't it? Will it? It's hard to tell. Sometimes everything seems pettier than the pettiest bene-bou or 'merchant's wife' bird; all I do is eat, drink, and do petty domestic tasks. Even those birds have plenty of crevices, light, all kinds of vast skies and grasses, but do humans have anything but labyrinths, last of the year and first of the year accounts?"—Malloban wanted to say all this and more, but his saying it came out in a language neither literary nor at home in their own mouths: this was not the ambrosial language of man's blood, water, sweat, and tears. He sensed this. This time he would speak without embellishments, in a thoroughly natural language of breath, blood, sweat, and nectar. After a stretch of forced and hollow talk, when the tongue of the public bazaar and the bridal chamber found its way into his mouth, Malloban heard the sound of snoring and sensed that he would never get along with Utpala— and yet he would have to get along somehow until death did them part. Ninety per cent of the husbands and wives of Bengal bear this very fruitlessness in their lives, but, in most circumstances, these husbands and wives are not able to appreciate this fact the way Malloban has. Those who do have no choice but to gather up the shards of a broken water glass and piece them back together so that they can drink: this male–female bond, this husband–wife business, this marriage thing, it's like a finely crafted glass, fragile and hard—it's bound to break, they're bound to drink water, no one will be given more than one glass; if one tried to forcibly take or steal another, that would be unsociable. True, the philosophers and scientists are working up a sweat, invoking annulment, remarriage, free marriage, but as far as the moneyed men of the moneyed classes are concerned, even if these solutions are idling at the back of their minds, they have little meaning; on the part of those like Malloban, the poor of the poorer classes, annulment and free marriage have no meaning at all. The collective bodies of lower-class society would burst their guts and die laughing like the folktale cat Majantali Sarkar at the sight of someone sloughing off one marriage only to slip into another one, or the nation going around pretending to be a well-meaning, scientifically-minded leader, determined to abolish the marriage bond and establish the rule of free intercourse among adult men and women. Will science ever fathom this free adult intercourse—even after it has determined the count of the stars of the sky, the sands of the netherworld? Will a ruling body of well-meaning scientists ever fully comprehend the benefit of this free adult intercourse? Never. But does it even exist, this kind of well-meaning scientific rule? It's nowhere to be seen. He's a man of the poorer class, this Malloban. There are heaps of men more wretched and downtrodden than he, and they are even worse off— but the problem of their stomachs has tidily suppressed all these other problems; the solutions to these problems, too, offer them a more careless or desperate or bold comfort— not unlike the comfort enjoyed, on another account, by the higher classes. But the problem is with middle-class people like Malloban. Is Malloban lower middle class—or middle middle class? Quite possibly he's a member of the lower middle class. But the problem has become so insufferably pervasive throughout the middle class—and nevertheless it's a sight worth seeing how middle-class Bengalis can keep house in peace and happiness if only they get their rice and cloth. Never mind the bond of husband and wife, even the bond of man and woman—in creation's manual of agents and actions, there is, after all, no mandate for peace and happiness. But in the love- and sex-lives of Bengali husbands and wives, there is happiness, there is peace, for one hundred per cent of them, thought Malloban morosely with a short laugh. Utpala is snoring, submerged in some primordial depth of the winter night—bidding farewell to Malloban with such facile celestialness, and yet against Malloban's own wishes, against his taste, in unlove, in the pull of desire, in excessive greed, in lust, he will have to keep circling back to the likes of Utpala, an indifferent, well-bred woman with a beautiful body and lowly common sense, until his own death, so relentlessly, so despicably, begging the girl to protect sometimes the domestic peace and sometimes the public good name, dragged toward her sometimes by covetousness, all too rarely by love.

In the sky there are many stars; outside it is very cold; inside the room a profusion of soundlessness, darkness like the scent of the black coat of time; outside, the sound of dew falling, or of time flowing by—there is no sandglass anywhere, only the murmuring whispering sound of the sand, trickling out of Utpala's cold conch-like ears and into the depths of Malloban's soul.

TWO

The upstairs room has an adjoining bathroom. The bathroom opens onto a sizeable terrace. That is, the terrace as a whole is not a bad size—but the other tenants felt compelled to divide it and keep the better part for themselves. Some lovely green tarpaulins have been hung up to make a marvelous partition. On that side, those people; on this side, a deck chair, two cane chairs, a three-legged stool, another wooden stool, a sewing machine, Monu's schoolbooks. Some days Utpala spends the entire morning dawdling there with the harmonium or the sitar.

She likes this place a lot.

Since the sun beats down hard on the terrace in the afternoon, she has to withdraw to her room then for a little while. But as soon as the sunlight begins to shift a bit, Utpala draws the deck chair into the shade of the tarp and settles down there. She hums, or sews; reads novels, makes Monu do her studying; plays the esraj.

Sometimes, in the evening, Malloban comes out on the terrace and sits quietly in a chair for a long time. Sometimes he calls Monu over and sets about teaching her, one by one, any number of things about history-

geography-earth, justice, humanity, the meaning of
human life—the first meaning—the middle meaning—and
especially the ultimate meaning. The girl doesn't always
like to have to listen to all these things, and for his part
Malloban doesn't even always like the girl—but often she
listens quite intimately; when she lifts her fluid eyes to his
face, there's no telling what thoughts are going through
her mind. Utpala often says, "That girl's got her father's
stubbornness." Monu is pleased to hear that. But it isn't
that Malloban dotes on the girl excessively; for his wife
too, he has the standard love and respect. But maybe it's
a mistake to think that it's for them alone that he has kept
himself alive, fit, successful. Much of the time, his heart
longs to float from sky to sky and harvest to harvest like a
muniya bird or a fieldmouse. He doesn't stay very long out
on the terrace; putting on a dhuti and shawl, he goes out—
he would like to go to the Maidan, but he goes to Goldighi
instead; stick in hand, he keeps circling Goldighi late into
the night, thinking various things—distancing himself from
his clerk's desk and from Utpala's husbandry—(but none
of these thoughts is very fully formed). He leads a variety
of fictional lives. Then, growing dispirited, he goes and
sits down on a bench, lights a cheroot; gets hungry; comes
back home.

Utpala never lets Malloban bathe in the second-floor
bathroom.

"You get the water all dirty in the morning, hurrying
through your bath before work. You, babu, will bathe in
the water tank downstairs—"

"But on the days I don't have to go to the office?"

"Yes, even on those days."

So Malloban bathes downstairs; now and then, even so, he takes his towel and clothes and heads for the upstairs bathroom.

"But I've only drawn one tub of water—it'll all get used up—"

"There's still water in the tap, after all," said Malloban.

"Monu's just about to take her bath."

"That's fine, let her get ready. In the meantime, I'll get my bath out of the way."

"What happened to the tank downstairs?"

"Not even the neighbors bathe there—they have a bathroom upstairs, that's enough for all of them."

"Oh, come on! It's like arguing with a dhenki. Their bathroom is practically the size of a reservoir. You can't compare theirs and ours—"

"They've got plenty of people too—but even so no one goes to bathe in the downstairs tank."

"Who's going to do that? Are there any men in their house? If there are any, they're tied to their women's sari-ends. How else would a man get into a woman's bathroom?"

Malloban grumbled a little and went down to the tank.

Another day, when he was going to take a bath, he said to Utpala, "Look, the water downstairs is really cold."

"Where will you find hot water in this cold weather?" Utpala said. "We've got a cook after all. Can't you get him to heat a kettle of water for you?"

"Of course I can," said Malloban, thinking a bit. "But it gets to be a very bad habit, bathing in hot water like that. It's unhealthy."

"What do you want then?"

"I won't touch your tub of water at all, I'll just sit under the tap for a bit."

"Don't give me that, bapu. Monu's just about to take her bath—"

"So let her come, she can come with me."

"She can come with you!" Utpala rolled her eyes dramatically. "Look at the old patriarch. No, no, there'll be none of that. Get downstairs—get downstairs, you."

"That's all you have to say to me?"

Malloban stood still for a moment, then went downstairs. From that moment until the time he left for work, he didn't say a single word to his wife—didn't say a word when he came home from the office either. But when it became clear that nobody cared, he had to loosen up. Even then, he saw that his wife was in even more of a huff than he had been—so he had to loosen her up too.

After all that, he still didn't make any headway.

One day, a holiday, he said to her, "No, you know, I can't bathe downstairs anymore."

Utpala turned a deaf ear to this remark.

"Do they change the water in that downstairs tank even one day out of fifteen? I'll get sick bathing in that rotten water."

"Listen to this shalgram," said Utpala, "If you don't take him by the ears and make him work, then foul water, floodwater, water of seven ghats, god knows what will come and eat the man. Can you just shut your eyes and ears and leave the job to cooks and servants? They're born with the habit of dodging work. Why would they change the water, what do they care!"

"So I should do it all myself, I should let out the stale water and sweep out the tank every day myself? I should draw fresh water myself?"

"If you can't get the servants to do it, then you'll have to do just that. There's nothing humiliating in that—" Utpala said, sewing. "It's for your own convenience, after all."

"So you're saying that I should clear the grate and drain the stale tank water myself in front of all the people who work for these two households?" Pacing back and forth, Malloban stopped short, seized with a mild agitation.

"Why not, you'll just clear it."

"And the maids will stand there and laugh?"

"Why would they, tell me? Where did you ever see such a depraved maid?"

"I have. But you, how would you see anything? You think you're very worldly, or what? There are all sorts of creatures on this earth! What have you seen?"

"Never mind, why would I need to know all that!"

Malloban said, "Oh, so that's it? You're too good for this world?"

Utpala, absorbed in embroidering a chemise, gave no answer.

"Here I am bathing downstairs," said Malloban, pacing again. "You think that's a great honor for you?"

Utpala, needle thrust between her lips, was turning the chemise over and over, examining her handiwork. She said, "You're so petty."

"Me?"

"You can take one word and blow it so out of proportion—"

"Upstairs there's a tap, there's a bathroom, and yet day after day I bathe in the tank like a janitor—what must the neighbors think!"

Utpala, taking the needle out of her lip, said with a sigh, "They don't go sticking their noses into your dirty laundry. They were born on this earth with a big heart. Are they going to fall down laughing at the sight of some lanky lout in front of the tank? Are they going to roll their eyes back in their heads and keel over at the sight of a man old enough to be their father?"

Malloban, still pacing back and forth, stopped in some arbitrary place and said, "The other day I heard Mejothakurun say, 'That clerk babu bathes in the servants' tank—does water go for the price of gold in Kolkata these days?'—She said all that, all that, ugh, the hairs on my head stood up when I heard it—"

"Who said that?"

"Mejothakurun."

"Well, a well-bred woman is bound to say something like that."

"She was right, after all."

"So what if she was right? Did you have to stuff the end of your dhuti in your mouth and creep away like a thief?"

"What was I supposed to do, go and pick a fight with other people's wives and maids? What are you saying, Utpala?"

Utpala had been sewing all along; she stuck the needle between her lip and teeth again and said, "You call her someone else's wife, all right, but those who say that kind of thing in front of other people's menfolk—"

Utpala stopped short of finishing the sentence poised on her tongue.

Malloban had ended up standing in the same place, he sat down on a torn couch stained with oil and sweat and said slowly, "Never mind. The main thing is, bathing like that—standing out in the open with all my body hair exposed, with people's wives and maids coming and going, winking and smirking—it doesn't suit me. Some of those women just plunk their elbows on the upstairs railing and stand there watching me bathe—as if I were a shivalinga getting a quick bath—or taking a dip at the beach."

Running the sewing machine, Utpala said, "So what is it you want to say—you're going to shut all the doors and windows, cover your head, and duck into the upstairs bathroom, and I, a woman, will have to go down to the tank and draw a crowd on the upstairs veranda, let their men have a peep at Kamikhye?"

"No, why would you do that?" said Malloban uncomfortably, as if he had suffered an especially vicious bite from the bugs that had been biting him ever since he sat down on the couch.

"Yes, yes, that would be best."

"You didn't understand what I said."

"Aare baba, I understand everything. I've seen my share of landowners' sons—even in the winter, in Aghran or Poush, if they find a pond or even a puddle, they jump right in with a splash and have their bath.It's a sight for sore eyes. And here you are harassing a woman just for a drop of water!"

Malloban got up, grumbling.

It was his day off. Besides the tank, there were plenty of other things to talk about. But who could he talk to? Any listeners? No sympathy, no humor. After walking back and forth on the terrace for a little while, muttering, stopping, and sitting down now and then, Malloban went into the room; sitting down in a chair, he said, "I bathed in a pond too, for seventeen or eighteen years of my life."

"Good for you."

"Weren't you talking about landowners' sons? But where am I going to find a pond in Kolkata, tell me?"

"Tanks are Kolkata's ponds."

"Fair enough. But I have to take my bath in a towel— there are women everywhere you look—"

"Oh, Ruplal Babu's such a delicate creature! His beauty will slip out at the slightest sneeze or cough! The women leave the chyanchra to burn in the kitchen and sneak out to get a glimpse of Ruplal Babu. The milk burns in the kitchen—they just crowd their bodies together like machpatori and stand there admiring the beauty of that sea of beauty—"

Malloban slowly went downstairs. He lay on his bed and thought: today he had the day off work, there were heaps of things to talk about—but Utpala will think he'd sat down and opened the hamper—a man at that. She has her ideas about women and men, that girl—in terms of both essential properties and proper conduct! Where did she get these ideas? Who taught them to her? Unlove—quite possibly unlove alone had taught Utpala to think like this.

Lighting a cheroot, Malloban thought: it's a mistake for a man to try to talk to women about anything subtler than the big slam-bang things of life, one has to wait patiently for the day they come to listen of their own accord. Would anything good even come out of that? Taking a few draws on the cheroot, Malloban thought—but Utpala will never come to him like that. He's seen twelve years go by. That woman, sweet or poisonous or cold as she might be—she's not the kind of bird to come and listen to words like the flesh of a custard-apple from the well-guarded green forest of his life. If she was dark and unattractive, then she would be unworthy of comparison to a Chamar woman. I'm making my home with a scavenger in the vain hope that someday she'll be like a bird in a custard-apple forest—wanting the bird that is not, I—

But Malloban quickly grew disgusted with the rhetorical uneasiness—the unnaturalness of his own stream of thought and figurative language. It's not quite that, it's something else. But what? Whatever it is, there's no easy pleasure in life— wanting to refine the coarse pleasures of eating, drinking, lying down, and sleeping, he's only made a muddle of it.

THREE

"You're earning two hundred and fifty rupees now—why don't you get rid of one stain on our honor."

"What do I have to do?"

"I'm not a fan of eating off leaves on the terrace," said Utpala.

"It's so nice though to eat out in the fresh air, while it's still light, picking out fishbones," said Malloban, looking at Utpala fixedly, solicitously, as if his glasses had slipped down to the end of his nose. "Isn't it a relief from dark drafty corners? Out in the light, on the terrace? Eating on the terrace is marvelous. It suits me marvelously."

"The terrace is always such a dump."

"But not for long?"

"When you're getting ready to face the day at the office, you just gulp down a mouthful and scramble up a tree, don't you—what do you know?—I sit here by myself and put up with all this mess, what else."

"Do the scraps sit out for a long time?"

"The maid makes eyes at Thakur, Thakur takes pinches of snuff from the maid's hand—and only then does he remember the scraps—"

"Is that so?" said Malloban, collecting a couple of black clouds on his face, "How long does he leave them out? Two or three hours?" After a little silence, Malloban said, "He's got a lot of nerve, in that case—" Malloban stared at her a little longer, thinking it over, and said decisively, "If we kick out this maid, that'll be the end of it."

"No, there's no need for all that."

"Didn't you just say she flirts with the cook?"

"Let her, what harm does that do us?"

"But that's not good."

"We're concerned with their work, why should we go poking our noses into their last rites?"

"But Bhadurani has a husband—and she's still fooling around with Thakur."

"I see you're a fine fool yourself!"

"Why?"

"All kinds of scandals go on among the lower castes."

"Lower castes? Bhadurani's a Brahmin's daughter."

"That may be. Fine then—Thakur is a Brahmin too—"

Thakur is a Brahmin too: to Malloban the matter seemed for a moment like a Chinese proverb, simple yet difficult, difficult yet simple; what is this simple matter—what does it mean—he could come up with nothing definitive. Baring his teeth stained with tobacco smoke—like those very teeth, in utter indescribableness, he remained staring at Utpala.

"All we have to do is stop eating on the terrace and start eating in the room on the north side—nice and spick and span, that room—"

"But that belongs to the other tenants—"

"No, dear, they've left that room."

"When did they leave it?"

"Yesterday."

Malloban thought a bit and said, "The rent isn't going to be cheap—"

"They want fifty rupees—I can talk them down to twenty," she said, looking at Malloban with a little sparkle of laughter.

Malloban lifted his eyebrows and said, "Twenty rupees additional expense?"

"But you got a raise."

"But all kinds of expenses have risen too. Why take on another one?"

"But it's impossible to eat on the terrace—"

Malloban was thinking: staring at Utpala as if his glasses had slipped down to the end of his nose, from amidst just some such unfathomable void, in unquiet singlemindedness and solicitousness.

"As soon as we get up from eating, the crows and sparrows come down and scatter the scraps all over the place, the clothes I hung up to dry on the terrace get fishbones stuck on them, get stained with potatoes, spices, turmeric, bird droppings . . . Krishna's honor is stained more than Radha's: stinking crabs, shrimp claws, chewed-up fibers, ants, flies swarming all over the roof, it's disgusting!"

"Couldn't we eat in the kitchen?"

Giving herself a slap with her right hand, maybe to squash a mosquito lurking in the lock of hair on her left cheek, Utpala said, "They're asking twenty rupees rent, are you going to put down the cash, or keep talking like a middleman? Have you ever been in the kitchen?"

"No, what's in there?"

"My bracelet and the bells from your feet."

Exhibiting a row of dirty teeth for an instant, Malloban shut his mouth immediately. Whether he had flashed a faint smile or just wrinkled his nose, there was no telling.

The room on the north side of the terrace was taken. Nice, shiny whitewashed walls, windows and door freshly painted green—lovely.

"There's been talk of your Mcjoshala coming to Kolkata; if he does come, then Monu and I can stay in this room—we can leave the big room to them—"

Malloban, stroking the stubble on his upper lip, was thinking the matter over and didn't answer.

For the time being, a long table was brought in and set up in the middle of the room—around it, three or four chairs. From morning tea until dinner, everything took place at this table.

One day, reading through a thin letter, Utpala said, "Mejda is coming."

"When?"

"It'll be a while yet, of course."

"This month?"

Setting the note aside, Utpala said, "Within a month and a half, with the family."

"Mejoshala has quite a few kids, doesn't he?"

"Three."

"Just three, but they're getting pretty big."

"Yes."

"Then space will be tight."

"We'll move into that dining room."

"You and Monu?"

"The two of us, for sure." With an expression as hard as the skin of a wisened tortoise, Utpala said nevertheless, "You can come too, we'll see how it goes."

Malloban, starting to articulate a word with great enthusiasm, caught himself and uttered something else: "How are you going to fit three people into that bit of a room?"

"I'll arrange for that. If we put in two cots, that'll do for the three of us. Even a cell will do for us. You've seen the inside of one in Dumdum jail."

Mistaken for satyagrahis in the midst of an unruly crowd, Malloban and Utpala, along with many others, had once been arrested and were stuck in jail—for two days—about six months ago.

"I've seen it all right," said Malloban, but in all this time, why hadn't a cot—even a camp cot—been put out for him in the big room on the second floor? If not that, why hadn't Malloban been allowed to sleep in that great big bed of Utpala's?

Storing up the sky-sized futility of his married life in a speck the size of a sesame seed, and still seeing the universe in that speck, Malloban was thinking with a slightly morose smile: Kankareshwari-Parameshwari: "queen of grit" rice in the Queen's jail . . . in jail we were squeezed into a crab hole. If your Mejda comes, the dining room will do. But why, when it's just you and me living in this house, is there no room for me in this big room on the second floor? In the downstairs room the heifer-calves pull the big goat's ear, if you don't keep me tethered with that tug-of-ear, your pastoral sleep doesn't come to fruition upstairs, I take it?

It was decided that the three of them would stay in the dining room on the north side of the roof, relinquishing the other two big rooms to Mejda and his family.

"Mejobouthan is not a bad person," Utpala said, "but I worry for Mejda. Mejda is a bit wedded to comfort, you know—"

"Like a hilsa of the river Padma, your Mejda."

"How's that?"

"Those fish can't bear a single moment of sunshine—"

"All right, all right, that's enough," said Utpala. "I was saying, if Mejda doesn't get a decent-sized room to himself, it's not going to work."

Malloban said, "I take it he'll stay in that big upstairs room by himself? That room's plenty big—and there's plenty of light and air. Fine, let him stay there."

"Yes, I'll give Dada that room."

"Where will your Bouthan stay?"

"She'll be in that room too."

"With your Dada?"

"Listen to you! Who else, Ramkanai?"

"Well, if Mejdi stayed in the downstairs room—"

"Bouthan will stay in the downstairs room? Why? What are you carping about?"

Malloban said, "The kind of comfort-loving man your Dada is, even if your Bouthan leaves him one room to himself and takes the kids into another room to sleep, he can still stay with her the whole day, or she can go and sit with him. There's no inconvenience for anyone in that arrangement—"

"But at night?"

"Then of course they'll each go to their own room to sleep."

"That's not going to happen."

"Why?"

"Without Bouthan close by, Mejda can't sleep. Mejda's in-laws tease him about it."

"It's certainly worth teasing about."

"How's that?" said Utpala. The flash of self-satisfaction on her face was extinguished.

"Does Mejda have some kind of illness?"

"No, nothing."

"A healthy man?"

"Mejda and Mejdi both. They're a match! It's been that way since the beginning. Are you planning to break it up now?"

"I was a great seller of shankha once," said Malloban with a bit of a laugh. "And your hands were soft as cream— so why was I never able to put any bangles on your wrists?"

Malloban's remark struck Utpala's ear like the soliloquy of some irrelevant character; she didn't even want to step on the shadow of that kind of confidentiality. As if she hadn't heard him, keeping up her own line of conversation, Utpala said, "A short letter came from Mejdi, from Pondicherry. After a month and a half, Mejda and Mejdi will come here from Pondicherry. The kids aren't in Pondicherry, they're somewhere close by—they'll pick them up from there and come here. What do you think about whitewashing our rooms?"

Malloban kept quiet; Utpala had given no answer to his very fresh remark; she hadn't even admitted she had heard it.

"We should paint the windows and doors beforehand," Utpala said.

"At our own expense?"

"Who else's? The landlord's?"

"No, no, he'll just look at us and laugh."

"He'll laugh?"

"The son-in-law's brother-in-law is coming, so the brother-in-law's sister's husband is painting the window-bars—Won't he laugh?"

It's a stretch to pay for the whitewash and paint job. And all that is hardly necessary. The walls are nice and clean, the doors and paneling not too bad either. Malloban isn't so flush with cash that he can afford this sort of decorating craze, but he doesn't go telling Utpala that. If he did tell her, she wouldn't understand. Of course, if Mejda did come and he spoke through him, she would understand, or through Mejdi; they're cool-headed; all the stops of their mental engines are working just fine. A mighty fine conjugal life they've set themselves up with, Malloban and his wife; as if staring at the fog from amidst the fog, Malloban remained staring at Utpala.

"Then the two of them will stay and sleep in this big room?"

"Yes."

"And the kids?"

"They'll sleep downstairs."

"They'll stay downstairs by themselves?"

"If we close the doors and windows, there's nothing to be afraid of."

Malloban said, staring at the fog, "Can't I go and sleep there?"

"In the middle of all those kids?"

"Yes."

Disinclination showed in Utpala's face like a hole in the void of time.

"No, how are you going to squeeze in there? All that overcrowding will only bother them."

"Then you can sleep with them," Malloban said.

"I can go sleep with them, sure. Maybe I'll have to do just that. Bouthan won't be able to come downstairs at night anyway."

Singing a song from a kirtan, Utpala went out onto the roof. First slightly bewildered, then benumbed, then coming to his senses, Malloban stayed sitting in the room for a long time; two kirtan songs were sung; by that time his feeling of disorientation, like a blind basket weaver in a bamboo grove, had mostly passed. Not because of the kirtan, of course! Just like that.

Letting out a heavy sigh, he went off toward the reservoir.

Walking around and around the reservoir, he thought many things; then, thinking a few too many things and seeing the 'notte' plants of the fairytale ending cropped limbless like Jagannath, he sat down on a bench and lit a cheroot.

FOUR

Two or three days later Malloban said, "Your Mejda and them will be staying quite a while then."

"Yes."

"A year or so?"

"No, six months or so."

"One thing occurs to me," Malloban said, "It wouldn't be a bad idea if we left this house and looked for a new one. A house with a few nice big rooms on the second or the third floor."

At that, her nose and eyes shining with happiness, Utpala said, "That would be lovely." Humming a bit, she said, "Have you seen a house like that somewhere?"

"No."

"It'll be hard to find."

"I'm looking."

"It'll have to be something in the fifty-rupee range, won't it?"

"You can figure I'd even give ten rupees more."

A few days later, Malloban came and said, "I've found a house."

"Where?"

"Over by Pathureghat."

"Oh dear, you went that far?"

"But it's a nice house."

"How many rooms?"

"Five. Four on the second floor, one on the third."

"Nice and big?"

"Yes."

"How much do they want?"

"Fifty."

"Fifty rupees is an awful lot."

"But five rooms."

"I got that—"

Stained red with dried traces of paan, Utpala's lips looked terribly pretty. Moving those lips, she said, "But we can't ask Mejda for anything."

"I know that."

"Even if he gives us something of his own accord, we can't take it." Malloban had a bit of a difference of opinion on that one.

Malloban said with a yawn, "You're right, how do we even manage on two hundred and fifty, if we throw away fifty just on rent—"

Utpala assured him in a low voice, "I can manage, of course—"

"Oh no, how will you do that! And there aren't so few of us—"

"If you sell off your gold watch, then we could make ends meet somehow—"

"I'm supposed to sell off my gold watch!" As if he were just about to let out a breath and found he could no longer do it, Malloban remained standing there, unmoving. "That one you got when we were married—" Utpala said, staring at Malloban's face.

But this face of Malloban's—a peculiar face, like a crushed pleat, as if it had just been ironed and was already crumpled—Utpala found it unpleasant to look at, and felt disgusted.

"My father bought you that watch for three hundred rupees. I'm telling you to sell it for the sake of that same father, for the sake of my brother's convenience. What else are you going to do with that watch, adorn your forehead with green beetle-wing?"

As if invoked by some agitated mantra such as "Come sun, beating down, I'll slay a goat for your renown," Utpala's eyes beat down into Malloban's like harsh sunlight; advancing with every word, Utpala almost fell on his face. Malloban slowly went downstairs and didn't come back up even for tea and porota.

A little while later Monu came back from downstairs and said, "Baba's gone out, Ma."

"What, he went out without his tea?" Tilting the teacup a little, she poured out the bit of tea that was in it, off the edge of the roof.

She said to Monu, "Will you eat a porota?"

"No, Ma, I feel like I've got heartburn."

"It makes me laugh to hear that a tiny little girl like you could get heartburn." Flinging two porota at a few crows on the roof, Utpala turned to look at Monu and said, "Heartburn! Who taught you that word—"

"But my chest is burning."

"They do call that heartburn, true enough. But who did you hear it from?"

"What do you mean, you say it all the time."

"I've said it?"

Sending Monu a sharp look, Utpala said, "Has anyone in my father's house ever had heartburn? Why would I say that?"

Monu kept quiet.

"Tell me straight out, where did you hear that word?"

"Dhet, I don't remember all that—"

"You don't remember. You've inherited your father's erudition, and you don't remember. It's spelled like it looks, you've sure got your father's stubbornness, child."

No matter how miffed Malloban had been, he showed up at home in time for dinner. Dishing out rice for the three of them, Utpala said, "You're awfully small-minded, tomar boddo khude mon—like Khudiram—not the Khudiram who was hanged—terribly greedy, that mind of yours."

"Mine?"

"You went off in a big huff without your tea?"

"Oh—tea—" Malloban laughed a bit through his nose—as if nothing had happened; as if the tea had entirely slipped his mind.

"The tea and porota just sat there—in the end the dogs and cats ate it—the body-eater's anger eats the body."

"No, no, not angry—who gets angry at food—I'm not that much of an idiot!" Malloban said, putting on a face like a wise man who has forborne anger for good, and turning up the sleeves of his panjabi a bit. "Let me have that plate of rice—"

Cutting a lime with a knife, Utpala said, "You don't miss being an idiot by much—"

Then, giving Monu a slap on the head, she said, "What are you doing nosing around there, sticking your face in the food like an oaf! Wretched girl, sit down—and she just stares at me shamelessly. That hereditary gluttony is already billowing up in her belly."

Malloban was wishing he could get up and leave this time too. But no one would learn anything from that. No one can be made into what they will never be. If he gets up in the middle of dinner and leaves without eating anything, he'll earn himself nothing but an empty stomach. If Utpala sticks with Malloban until his death—she'll stick with him just like this; there's no reformative or scientific wisdom that can set these womenfolk straight—even in the hands of America or Russia; no individual has the lakhs, the crores, the inexpendable time on hand to turn coal into diamonds.

Monu came and sat down in a chair facing her father. Malloban couldn't find the strength to console her. He didn't even bother to look at her. Here he is sitting beside the girl—Malloban's heart began to grow heavy as if exhausted from the jagged acceleration of a khemta dance. He had become a father himself—he had married—with lowly, ugly violence, he had strewn the seeds of life. His mind felt singed just thinking of it. If one creates a bird and abandons it in the dark of a draw-well—a sort of restlessness stirred up inside him. Malloban was thinking: he should have stayed single; he would have read the newspaper, gone to the office, strolled around the reservoir, gone and sat in the front row at meetings and associations, especially theosophical associations, he would have been a freemason, stayed up all night reading everything from detective novels to the minutes of Calcutta University, various commissions' reports, blue books, whatever came to hand, he would have thought, appreciated—how splendid life would have been then.

Involving a female in his life—dirtying himself with the meaning invested in this involvement, in soured milk and slime and stupidity, in disgorged bile and fire and dissatisfaction, what has he become?

After a little while, quietly dishing out the rice, dal, and vegetables into plates and bowls, Utpala said, "Your parents gave you a fine upbringing—"

"Why, what happened, what did you see me do?"

"Why else would you act like such a glutton?"

"Glutton?" On the point of flinging the plate of rice at Utpala, Malloban found himself restrained by some Vaishnavite force; for a couple of minutes he could understand nothing at all through the blood mounting to his head in murderous rage.

Slowly his mind cooled down.

"If not, then—" Utpala said.

"What have I done?"

"You just pulled up your sleeves and grabbed for your plate—even when you could see plain enough that the bowls of rice, dal, vegetables, and fish weren't ready yet. The hair on your neck has gone white, and you still slaver like a mad dog—just slaver!" There were tons of things Malloban was itching to say, but trying to brush off the matter lightly, he said, "I was hungry, so I asked for my plate." "Horses get hungry too, that's no excuse for making a person's table into a stable," said Utpala, shoving the plate of rice in Malloban's direction. "When a man's past twenty or twenty-five, all that bravado runs its course—boys grow up into splendid menfolk—splendid. Girls become women at seventeen or eighteen—but even at forty-two, you can't control yourself."

Malloban was eating, his head bent and slightly tilted away like on the winter solstice.

Utpala said, lifting a bite to her mouth, "If it's written on your brow that it's not going to happen, then the writing won't be mopped off with the sweat of that brow—that writing doesn't come off with sweat or blood."

Monu wasn't getting much of this; Malloban wasn't saying much of anything; there was complete silence in the dining room for a few moments; each engrossed in his own thoughts, they kept on eating, sprinkling salt, squeezing lime, lifting the water glass to the mouth, tilting the bowl of vegetables.

"But what happened today when you came back from the office?" Utpala said, as if the heat of her anger just refused to die down.

Modifying his table manners a bit in an effort to eat more politely, Malloban said, "Nothing happened."

"You're lying flat out!"

"What could have happened?"

"You went out without your tea, that's what happened."

"I'd had my tea out."

"Where?"

"At a shop."

"Who treated you to tea?"

"Who could have treated me?"

"You bought it out of your own pocket?"

"That's how I prefer to do it—"

"Your friends have it easy enough. After all, who would empty their pocket plying this regular Ganesh with egg-chops?" Utpala said. "They spend their money all right—and freely—but only according to the man—they size him up good—"

Utpala looked Malloban up and down in hard silence for a few moments.

"They don't treat you to a single cup of tea. What, aren't you allowed to touch water outside of the house?"

"They don't treat Baba to tea?" Monu said. "How about yogurt or sweets?"

Malloban was soundlessly spearing a potato.

"The few invitations we get are from your in-laws' house. Even Lochona Dom blesses her son-in-law on Jamai Shasthi—it's a formality. After sitting around for forty-two years in this big world, the man is half-blind in the company of men—just like a mole or a bat—"

Moistening her throat with a little water, Utpala said, "No one calls, no one comes, there's no commotion, no company or chitchat in your room—no sound of khol-kartal, kirtan, mujra—not a single human being ever makes an appearance—even if you call, they don't come. But who can make a deaf man hear? Is it any use showing the right hand to a lefty?"

Malloban was eating. Monu was listening, laughing, forgetting, not understanding, negligently, with a look of distaste, now and then she would start nibbling again—

"Ever since our wedding day, I've been seeing those two chairs down in Clerk babu's room. He sits in one of them himself, and he sits in the other one himself too. Someone or other used to come for a half-akhrai now and then—oh, Abhiram Sarkhel; but then he was driven away, as if his visits were some kind of attack."

Utpala let out a turbid sigh. But it's in Malloban's chest that the pain strikes deepest—not because he has no friends, but because that kind of a grimace, that kind of a jab has been made at what little subtle meaning there is in the silence of his life. Nonetheless, when Utpala's no longer out of sorts, when she's still—then all the strange refractory words that she has rattled out all her life, the foolishness of all of that, keep her silent—so silent it seems as if, above the sea, across the earth, out of everyone's reach, beyond an endless "I am becoming," "I will become," she's sitting in the thick of some eternal "I have become." But now it's the other kind of Utpala, unfortunately, with this timeworn way of hers.

Taking a piece of lime from a nearby plate and squeezing it onto the dal, Utpala let out such a sigh, like a conveyance for aversion and futility; the sigh is correct according to its own laws—correct in such an unadorned way that it seems as if, surfacing from some abyss, it's diffused before it can be expended for some crude use; a person's soul quakes just hearing it.

Malloban no longer bothered trying to enhance the flavor of the dal by breaking a raw chili and rubbing it on the side of his plate. Eating is now irrelevant. What is he going to do with this woman? All of Utpala's piquant remarks, apathy, rivalry, and deep sighs, Malloban's failure and his own inexhaustible sighs (a kind of deadly cough has settled in Malloban's chest, not outwardly discernible, and Utpala has never suspected it) are thrashing about in the quiet air of the rooms. What will come of these rooms and this air? What will he do with this woman?

"The handful of people who come to see you, it's impossible to look them in the face."

"Why?"

"They're not bad to look at, but their blood gives off a limy stink. Isn't there any remedy for it?"

"I don't know."

"That's why I don't speak to them."

"They sit and talk with me behind the arum plant. I don't think they've ever even seen you."

Utpala said, "You get through the monsoon just fine with your umbrella of arum leaves, with a couple of crabs on top. You're just like them. Are you acquainted with any other girl besides your wife?"

"What would I get out of that?"

"I knew it. What I think about your friends, other people's wives must think the same thing about you," Utpala said, pushing the water glass around with her food-soiled hand. "Chhi, how disgusting!"

"No, there's nothing disgusting about it—we lead two different lives, that's all."

"In such a big world, not even one girl has felt the need to care for you—not love, not affection or respect, not fondness or sympathy, nobody has anything at all to give Clerk babu. Oh, I'll have to give you everything myself, I suppose. Like Lakshmi's goody-basket!" Utpala said. Her voice rising as she spoke, Utpala said at the top of her voice, "If I could go halves on my responsibility for you, even with a prostitute, then I wouldn't be so stifled—"

Hearing that, Malloban didn't start up, didn't start laughing; he was hungry; Utpala didn't intend to not let him eat, but that's how it went. The things on the table could have fed four or five, but Monu isn't even managing to eat up her little portion; and the two of them have stopped eating; they've chosen a splendid time to start fighting tooth and nail.

Monu had put her head on the table and was falling asleep. Malloban had picked up a lime peel and was doodling with it on his plate, quiet.

"I'm the daughter of a Hindu household, I'm forced to believe a lot of things—"

Malloban was drawing swastikas, auspicious symbols of domestic well-being, on his plate with the lime peel— one—two—three—he didn't say a word.

"When it comes to belief and disbelief, every human being is independent—but having been born in such a conservative household and ending up in such an eccentric one, I've lost that independence—"

"What is it you're forced to believe?"

"That this marriage was meant for me, that I couldn't have prevented it in any way—"

"Oh, that—" Wiping out the swastikas on his plate, Malloban was trying to draw the twelve tails of Genghis Khan's emblem—perky yak tails.

"But this is just custom," Utpala said, "It's not truth. It's not at all truth."

As if she were Galileo saying, I don't believe at all that the earth is square, I don't believe at all that the earth is standing still. As he drew the tail of Genghis' yak, lifting his face once to look at the unbending Galileo, Malloban felt amazed—as if there's some kind of aura surrounding Utpala—as if she's engaged in ascetic exercises for the supreme truth of science—engaged in struggle.

"I could have not married you. That's the truth," Utpala said.

"That's what I think too. Throwing a bird in the cage and telling it to think that cage is truth, that's meaningless. The sky is truth, the nest is truth to the bird—"

This time Utpala turned her attention to the rice and vegetables and said, "I was saying just that—"

After eating a couple of bites, she said, "I could have married Anupam Mahlanabish, after all—"

With the lime peel and his nail, Malloban has succeeded in drawing the yak-tail-emblazoned emblem of Genghis— he has drawn exactly twelve tails—on the plate; lifting his eyes and looking at her he said, "Who's Anupam Mahlanabish?"

"I should have married someone like that. That would have been truth, but it's hard to see the face of truth in this world."

Staring at Genghis' tails on the plate, Malloban said, "Oh, yes, Anupam Mahlanabish; I've heard of Mahlanabish. Anupam Mahlanabish, Dhiren Ghoshal, Noshu Chaudhuri—I think they're all martyrs of the Baleswar battle, of the fish-market bombs, of the Kakori case, of the Chatgaon armory raid, but no, that's not it, those are other people, materialists—you've talked about them many times. It would have been right for you to marry one of them, it would have lasted. But that didn't happen. But just because of that, because you're the daughter of a Hindu household, it's proper that it didn't happen, and what did happen is truth—you can't not accept that, that's what you're saying?"

Lifting his face from the plate of food and looking at Utpala, Malloban said, "You're saying you can't not accept it. But actually, you're not accepting it. Maybe your blood's disease-eating cells are accepting it, but the white cells are not, your soul is not."

Utpala, letting out a big sigh, started to say something and didn't. Malloban was mixing the fish stew with rice and squeezing lime juice on it; throwing away the lime peel, he said, "Who's going to make Hindu wives understand that there's no more constant scientific truth than this. Even if a thousand years go by, will they understand?"

Utpala liked this conclusion. She said, "Everyone called Anupam Mahlanabish a terrorist. He looted the mail and the train, he looted the armory, what didn't he do—and how he rotted in jail to make the country independent. One time, Anupam had been sentenced to be hanged, but even I don't know how it got rescinded when he was still a member of a terrorist group."

Genghis was a very big Khan, Malloban was thinking, and the Mongols were awesome people, but in the mud of reasons it was Kublai Khan who stood out like a lotus stalk.

"Oh, you never told me you were involved in a terror plot."

"What would I get out of telling you?" said Utpala. "That's all over now. It was a long time ago."

"Anupam Babu's hanging was rescinded? Did he get the Andamans?"

"No."

"Not even that? How did that happen?"

"The India Secretary can tell you that. He didn't even get jail time."

"Not even jail?" After wiping the whole emblem off the plate, Malloban has almost managed to eat up the fish stew and rice; the plate is almost clean again; he'll be able to draw pictures again—he'll draw a portrait of another big Khan—of Kublai.

"Not even jail? Anupam Babu had become an informer, it seems?"

"I don't know."

"But since he became an informer, didn't you feel less attracted to him?"

Utpala bent her neck and said, cutting a lime with a knife, "The terrorists said Anupam was a spy. Maybe he was. Maybe they said that because he wasn't hanged."

"Spy?" Malloban said with mild agitation, "That's even worse than an informer. Or is an informer worse than a spy? Spy?"

"Whether Anupam is doing swadeshi, or loading swadeshis into the government boat—I didn't think of any of that when I fell in love with him. He's a spy, is he?" Pushing away the fog from within her own gaze, looking clear-eyed at Malloban, and then turning her eyes away, Utpala gave a laugh mottled with derision and depression and said, "He might well be a spy. He might even be an informer. That doesn't make any difference to me. That's not how I form a bond with a man. It's not about water, there are huge amounts of water in ponds, rivers, seas, but is there that water—that crystal-clear rainwater?"

No, that there isn't. Not because Anupam is an informer, but just because he's Anupam, he is cloud-water. Glancing up at the high-power lightbulb above his head and dazzling his eyes, Malloban was thinking: it's because he and Utpala are part of a Bengali Hindu family that their conjugal bond has lasted twelve years. For these twelve years, in the densely woven boinchi-thorn, rattan-spine, moonfish-bone jungle

of Utpala's disinclination and distaste, Malloban has flown
his own deeds and desires like a blind bird on its dying
breath. What porcupine-impertinence, cockatoo-mischief,
civet-aggrievedness, cat-grimaces, cobra-fangs, and tigress-
paws this woman has. But if, facing those paws, one did
not behave like a doe or a wild cow but took an aggressive
stance like a royal tiger, she would fly like a peahen from
branch to branch in some magic jungle, like a new bride
setting up house in an invisible world, this girl; or else
she would fall dead at one's feet like a mynah—with both
yellow feet pointing up at the sky. In this life of mine, what
I wanted didn't happen, what I feared tumbled down into
greater fear, into greater grief—Malloban was thinking.
But I—thinking it through—I, a man, can cut across this
road, not even because I can reach some philosophical exit,
but just like that; I didn't end up with the same grotesque
failure and pain that's in Utpala's life. Monu and Utpala
finished eating, rinsed their mouths, cleared the table, and
went away. Malloban lit a cheroot. Leaving the dining
room, walking—standing a moment or two out on the
terrace, swallowing up with one glance, with an expansive
hawk-gaze, the igneous clusters of the winter night sky—
he went and entered Utpala's room. When with drag
after drag the cheroot has begun burning nicely, smoke is
flying, there is smoke coming out of Malloban's nose and
mouth—Malloban's mind had gone off who knows where,
now it became attentive again. He saw that the light in
his wife's room had been put out—darkness on all sides;
hanging up the mosquito net, Utpala had lain down, fallen
asleep perhaps. Malloban felt like lying down there inside
Utpala's mosquito net, inside the quilt. But he would have

to leave the splendid cold and darkness of this room and go downstairs.

The mouth of the cheroot had filled up with ash, he tapped it out and went downstairs.

The next morning while drinking tea at the table, Utpala said to Malloban, "What did you eat at the tea shop yesterday?"

"Tea and biscuits."

"Nothing else?"

"No."

"That gold watch Baba gave you, it didn't cost three hundred—it was four hundred, the price was written in my notebook, I saw it. Nowadays, the value of gold has risen—maybe it'll sell for two hundred. If we had that money in hand—Mejda's coming with the family—it would be convenient for them and for us too. But you're so selfish, you're only willing to husk your own rice."

Utpala hadn't taken even one sip of tea yet. This time, finishing half the cup of tea in four or five swigs and pushing the cup to the side a bit, she said, "Is that all, just because I told you to sell the watch, you got in a huff and went and ate at the tea shop. What is this—higgle piggle—higgle piggle—clucking his tongue like a girl because I brought up the matter of selling the watch—is this a man? What kind of man are you? That kind of man should marry a secondhand girl."

Utpala spoke in a cold, calm, compassionate way—but not without a suppressed sting. Malloban's eyes grew tender: Utpala really has a good heart, this tiny concern for her brother is true from root to tip; if, instead of me, any other person—whomever her white blood cells desired—if she found him, then the clear propensities of this woman's heart and soul would open a hundred paths—with ease, with ease—

Thinking this, Malloban closed his eyes and kept sitting there somehow occultly, with a face like a shamkol stork: someone with secret designs would never let the gold watch out of his hands. Malloban sensed this too, that he seemed like such a person now.

"I'll have to sell my own gold necklace. In our father's household, it's our practice that if there's anything that would be useful to other people, we don't keep it as capital—we distribute it, circulate it. But I'm becoming something else. Twelve years out of my father's house. The cow's piss got in the milk—why wouldn't it curdle?"

Malloban's surge of emotion—that which had entranced him—was ebbing at an opportune time; only some of what Utpala was saying entered his ears as sound waves; his mind had become all ears—not Utpala, not even Malloban himself, but Malloban's mind's absence of awareness approached perfect silence: what is she saying? Sell the watch why don't you, sell the watch, sell it, won't you, do it; do it, won't you, do it, do it. Is it only today he's sold the watch? Almost three years ago, to satisfy yet another of Utpala's demands for money, he'd had to sell the watch. She knows that very well. But still, pretending not to know—as soon as the price of gold goes up, she starts clamoring to sell that same gold watch: like an egret torn from some other pair, so ill-paired is this woman in Malloban's life.

Of course, Malloban does have another watch on hand, not a gold one. Will he have to sell that? No, that's not it. Only by selling again and again the gold watch that the father-in-law had given his son-in-law, Malloban will have to look after his father-in-law's son and his family in his own house, will have to allow his father-in-law's daughter to enjoy the perception that everything is unequivocally happening on the money of his father-in-law's daughter's father.

That's how it is, isn't it? What do they call this? The paternal bond? Or is it that the bird torn from her mate is lost in a shoreless, unfathomable void, and so her brother seems closer to her than her societal Sakshigopal—the paternal bond becomes activated? No, that's not right, Malloban was thinking, it can't be apprehended in any scientific pattern. Utpala is beyond science.

FIVE

One day Utpala climbed into a car of her own accord and went with Malloban to see the house in Pathureghat. She didn't like the look of it. And no other house was ready at hand. So it was decided that once Mejda's family came, Malloban would go and stay a while in a "mess."

Malloban sold his own remaining wristwatch and a few gold buttons (he had been keeping them hidden in a box) and gave the four hundred rupees he got for them to Utpala. She didn't have to sell the gold necklace.

All this made Utpala quite content. One day, a Sunday, she said to Malloban, "Monu's been saying for a long time she really wants to go to the zoo. I haven't been for a long time either. Come on, let's go today."

The three of them got into a tram. When they came close to Khidirpur Bridge, Malloban bundled his family off the tram.

"Great! Where is Alipur? You just got down in the middle of the way—"

"We'll have to go through this little bazaar, it's just a three-minute walk."

Walking through the Khidirpur bazaar, Utpala wrinkled her nose and said, "Ugh! Through this bazaar full of chickens and goats—isn't there any other road in Kolkata!"

Monu said, "It smells like goats, Baba. What a stink of piss, ick! Look over there, they're cutting up a goat—"

"Don't look over there, Monu—"

"If we had even a small Austin car, would the stench of all these drains and gutters, mud and piss ever get to us, Monu?"

"When I grow up, Baba will buy a car," said Monu.

"The car would stop right outside the gates of the zoo," said Utpala. "We'd get out right there." Utpala let out a sigh, but a sigh just as light, insubstantial, and aimless as the stirring of the float of a fishing line nibbled by a shrimp. Entering the zoo, Utpala said, "Why is it so cold? I'm chilled to the bone."

"Unfold your shawl and wrap it snugly around you, Pala."

"No, I'll keep it folded. It's not cold enough in Kolkata to put on a shawl in the middle of the day." Walking, she said, "It's no use wasting money on these things. Why did I even bring it, what if it gets lost!"

"Hand it to me."

"No, I'll keep it."

Turning to Monu, Utpala said, "Do you want to see the monkeys, Monu—"

The shaggy head started dancing, "Yes, I want to see them."

"You're a monkey yourself. We'll have to lock you up in a cage from now on. Monu re, you were born as my daughter!"

She said to Malloban, "Come on, let's go to the monkey house."

They all went there together.

Monu said, "See Ma, they're putting out their hands for bananas; Ma, buy some bananas to give them."

"You want to give them bananas or elephants? Let them digest what they're eating."

"Why, can't they digest? Do they get heartburn?"

Utpala said to Malloban, "These animals' jaws just keep going and going, don't they get stomach ulcers and so on?"

"What do I know!"

Monu was staring at the monkey cages, completely overcome with emotion; suddenly Utpala took hold of her hair bun, gave it a tug and said, "If I could shove you in there, that would be great."

Giving it another sharp tug, she said, "Why were you born from a human belly, tell me."

Turning to Malloban, Utpala said, "Come on, let's go see the tigers."

But the stench kept her far back from the tiger cage. She didn't even go look at the tigers. Utpala's guts were turning somersaults. She said, "That's enough zoo. Come on, let's get out of here."

Monu said, "I didn't even get to see the tigers. That's why we come to the zoo, to see the tigers."

But no one paid her any attention.

Malloban said to his wife, "Here you just came to the zoo, and now you want to leave already? Come on, let's see the birds at least."

"Are birds anything to look at? We see them night and day, after all."

"No, no, not those kinds of birds—"

"I've seen all the birds. I don't have any desire to see them."

"All you see in Kolkata is crows and sparrows; shoral, partridges, cockatoos, mackaws, so many kinds of geese, herons, flamingos, dhanesh, shamkol—come on, don't you want to see them—come on—"

"The dhanesh you're showing me night and day . . ."

"Me?"

"Just as a cockroach turns into a glassbeetle, so the shamkol turns into a dhanesh—" With that, Utpala started snickering . . .

The three of them went together to see the walrus.

Monu said very pathetically, "I didn't get to see the lion," and she began to declare her pain repeatedly, desperately, to her parents. "I want to see the lion. Where's the lion? There, a lioness is calling!"

But nobody bothered to listen to what she said.

The walruses were in the middle of a pond—very low down. Walls on all sides. A white man was tossing them herring or something. Utpala shouted out, "Ooh, look how much fish they're eating."

"Why wouldn't they eat—they've got bodies like elephants."

"It makes me shudder."

"Why?"

"There they go eating bucket after bucket of fish."

"Of course."

"Won't they get dyspepsia?"

Malloban laughed a bit, curling his lip, and said, "Yes, dyspepsia."

Monu's head didn't reach over the wall; she couldn't see anything. She kept on whining at her parents, "Hey, where are the fish? How are they eating fish? Are walruses like crocodiles? Hey, where are the walruses?"

But those same parents who had been married according to the auspicious union of the stars did not take their daughter's words into account.

Furrows had come out on Utpala's brow and cheeks, making her beautiful face look ugly; evidently she had aged; she said wearily, "This is your zoo!"

"Why, it's not so bad."

"No! We'll never come here again."

"I like it a lot."

"Among the things to be seen, I wanted to see the tigers and lions. But, god, how it stinks—who can get close!"

"Why tigers, it's the birds you should see."

"Your taste differs from mine. Am I supposed to see the world through the eyes of a shamkol stork? If so, then birds would seem best to me—I would like the shamkol best of all—"

"What would be so bad about that?" Malloban said, as if standing in a separate world of symbols, mysterious to this woman of the material world.

"It didn't happen, did it?"

"It will in your next life."

"A shamkol in my next life! Oh brother!" Utpala shuddered and said, "No thank you, no life at all would be better than that. If I am reborn, I'll be a peacock and fly off to that jungle over by Gorakhpur—"

"I take it Mahlanabish Moshai is selling sharbatidoi over there. Fine, fine, go. Come on, let's take a look at the parakeets and the partridges—"

Monu said, "What's a partridge, Baba?"

Malloban didn't answer, he stared at Utpala and said, "Come on, why are you standing there? Let's go. White-breasted water hens, falcons, shikras, royal shamkol storks—let's see them all—let's see them all."

But Utpala was in no hurry at all. Not even bothering to look at Malloban, "I'll have to rest a bit—oh dear. Both feet are hurting—my back is broken—oh god!"

The three of them sat down on top of a flattish patch of grass under a tree.

As soon as she had sat down, she got back up and said, "There you go sitting everybody down on the grass, and look, there's a bench over there."

"I'd rather sit on the grass than on a bench."

"Grass makes me itch," said Utpala. She went and sat down on the bench by herself and said, "If so many people are sitting on benches, it's clearly because they like them." Then Utpala said to herself, "There are so many people around here, I fit in with them all so well, and yet with the people of my own household, it's like the flood tide of the Ganga called the 'bullfight.' On the grass, my skin gets scratched, my sari gets dirty, I have to wallow in the nectar from the feet of Muchis and Muslims—and yet they've all sat down, making like grass-cutters—grass!—If they don't get their grass, it's no go. Are you going to bind up bales and bales of grass, you father and daughter—" Utpala started rattling on—

Utpala had sat down on a bench ten feet or so from Malloban, but Malloban began to feel more strongly at every moment: to get rid of this little gap—if it's really possible to get rid of it—there will never come a call from Utpala's side. Besides that, on the bench it isn't grass within grass,

Monu and I as grass—in the waves of grass; the bench isn't even made of grass-tree wood—nor of paddy-tree wood; there's no wood like that anywhere; there's woody wood; with all that grass around, what frightful benches of woody wood all around.

Utpala said, "Come on, let's get out of here. Prakash Babu was supposed to come over this evening."

"You won't go see the birds?"

"I won't go without seeing the lion," said Monu.

"By the way, that bunch of fan-tailed pigeons sitting around that table over there, who are they?"

"I don't know them. I've never seen them before!" Malloban said, not even looking at the girls.

"See how they've tied their saris to show a half a foot of belly, and that stylish lock of hair hanging down by the ear. They're all unmarried, guaranteed. Really, girls who haven't married, they're the ones who have fun—" With that, Utpala turned her face and stared as if to swallow the girl with her eyes.

Malloban didn't like it. "Don't look over there, bapu! They're eating tea and scones. Why are you eyeing them, Pala."

For a few moments, Malloban kept completely still, staring at the white stalks of the grass; for a few moments he played with Monu's curly hair; after that he looked over at Utpala and saw that she was still gaping at the girl like a cow taking a huge bite of grass!

"Come and sit here—on this soft grass."

"Come on, let's get up now."

"Where will you go?"

"What will we gain by sitting here any longer?"

"Your feet are hurting, you said—will you drink some tea?"

"No. The pain has subsided."

"Come on, next to those girls there's another table empty—"

"No, take me somewhere else."

Turning back to look at the girl as she walked, Utpala said, "I thought today I would come out without putting a sindur-tip on my forehead—"

"Why?"

"Is all that always necessary?"

"Yes, that custom has gone out of fashion," said Malloban. "What's the use of going around with all those 'tips' and things."

"If I hadn't come out with this splotch of sindur, then what would these girls think, tell me—"

Malloban, thinking this and that, said, "They'd think something or other. I'll die in defense of thinking."

"Maybe they'd think you were my uncle or uncle-in-law—"

"If they could think I'm your household treasurer or purchasing clerk, then maybe there would be some gain in that—"

Tearing off a burr and making it into a toothpick as he walked, Malloban said, "That boy who went abroad and learned to skim milk—goes around in sahebi clothes all the time, doing sahebi things, that skim milk saheb, that Motin Chaudhuri of ours, dear—if you could have brought him along, then they'd sure watch you like hawks. That's their nature, after all. You've come to make a round of the zoo with a fabulously rich man like me—what is there to see in that. Who's going to look twice?"

"Who's Motin Chaudhuri?"

"Aha, I just said he came back from abroad after learning to skim milk."

"To lift butter out of milk?"

"Yes, yes, the butter-lifting saheb—"

"I would come with him to the zoo—what do you mean?"

"I was just saying—something to say—"

"You're such an idiot."

"I was giving an example—"

They were not heading for any destination, they didn't have a thought for what direction they were going, they were just walking around in the winter afternoon on the wispy-thin grassy fields of the zoo—on roads and unroads.

"You're earning two hundred and fifty now. How much will your salary be before you retire?"

"Two hundred seventy-five—three hundred—"

"Not more than that?"

"No!"

Utpala was thinking. Stopping in the middle of her thought-path, she said, "On a salary of two hundred fifty rupees, can't you afford to wear anything but a neckerchief and coat?"

"Why not? I could wear dhuti-panjabi! Nowadays plenty of people do!"

"Not that, I was talking about a hat and tie. Why don't you wear them? Then again, would they suit you if you did? It would look somehow out of place. Why is that so?"

"Why?" Malloban said, biting into the stalk of grass in his hand with his teeth, "Sugar is sweet and salt is salty! Isn't that so, Utpala—that's why it's so."

They went on in silence for a little distance. Nobody hears anything Monu says, nobody listens to any of her complaints—that's why she's shut up long ago.

Utpala said, "That bristly beard—you look like I don't know what—why didn't you shave before going out?"

"Suddenly this morning you said you want to see the zoo—where would I find the time?"

"Is that it! For that matter, what would you shave with—where would you find a razor!"

"Men who really shave their beards, they can't stop stroking their cheeks even when they're burning their first wives in the cremation ground—"

"They do, do they?"

"To see if they've shaved or not."

They aren't going out of the zoo—they aren't looking at anything—they aren't sitting anywhere—they're walking slowly as if they're pacing—mostly on top of the grass. Where are they going—why are they going—even if they haven't lost their way, no one thinks to ask anyone. Monu wasn't saying a word. Her feet were burning, her heart was palpitating, her tongue had dried out long ago. But no one responded to anything she said, no one gave her any encouragement, so she couldn't say anything to anyone. Monu had fallen behind a bit; the two of them stopped for a moment to wait for her. Monu caught up.

Malloban was not managing to kick out his feet as he walked in precisely the style Utpala preferred. As if Malloban's two legs just wouldn't straighten out the way

Utpala wanted them to—that beauty of footstep, that measure, that firmness, it was all beyond him. As they walked, they ended up by the tiger house again. From above the cage, raw meat was being flung down with great thuds to feed the animals—

"If you want to see how they eat meat, come over here."

Utpala said, shaking her head, "I'm going to leave now."

Reassuring herself as she walked, Utpala said, "My older brothers—Mejda, Chorda—they're not like you, they never gangle around like that."

She looked in front of her and saw two huge elephants standing there—nearby branches and leaves had been cut down and laid in a heap; the elephants were dragging them bunch by bunch with their trunks and eating them.

Monu said, "Did you see, Baba, how they pull the bananas with their trunks and throw them into their mouths?"

A little Muslim boy was giving out bananas—five or six elephants, but only ten or twelve bananas; but the elephants have shame, their propriety is a sight to see; they're standing close together, but no one's trying to snatch another's share, they content themselves with whatever offering falls to their lot; and then it's back to the branches.

Malloban was watching, fascinated; he said, "They understand life better than humans. And their capacity for withstanding the hardship and tedium of life is no less than that of a Chinese or Indian monk. Really, a thousand or two thousand years ago, they stood in all the grand public places of China and India; they've seen, heard, protected— that's given them a sense of the laws of dharma and karma, it seems."

Utpala was not reassured to hear this. Looking at the elephants' ears like winnowing trays and faces like old grannies, she had a confused sense of curiosity, aversion, and dull disquiet. She said, "Never mind, I've had enough. Let's go."

As he started walking, Malloban said, "But once you go out, you won't be able to come back in."

"I don't want to come back in. I don't think I'll ever come back to this place."

"Come on, let's buy some chickpeas and go to the cockatoo house. They'll eat the peas and read co-cka-too."

"Some birds can really read well. Can all of them read?"

"If you teach them, they can. Let's go."

"Forget it."

"There are cockatoos of all colors, with lovely furry feathers. If you look at their wings, their whole bodies seem to have sprung from fire—they're all playing in the midst of fire—playing from fire to fire, one day they'll blend into the blue of the sky—come on—come on—"

Utpala just stood there; pointing with her finger, she said, "There's that table, those same four girls were sitting there, weren't they? Right there?"

Before Malloban could say anything, Utpala said, "Where did they go?"

"They left."

"I didn't see them anywhere inside the zoo."

"They've gone out."

"They went out so soon?"

"They came in a long time before us. They're done with looking, listening, fooling around—why would they keep sitting there. Are they supposed to sit around all day for a prostitute's son's annaprashan?"

Malloban's comment about annaprashan was nothing; chewing the word over once with hardened teeth and jaws, Utpala brushed it away; she said, "I saw that girl, with jilipi syrup in her every bend. They're going all out, getting all sweet and shiny, what a fountain of fun—the whole time; they're not dropping dead—not like me."

"I take it you'd be saved if only you could have fun like them?"

"How would that be?" Utpala said, letting out a sigh as if freed from all desires.

"Fun means amusement—"

"Amusement, you say—"

"Real amusement—"

"You mean, happiness?"

Spitting betel juice on the grass, Malloban said, "Oh, all those girls! They're sluts—a whole clan of true happiness and amusement. And still people think about them! Still bother to gossip about them!" Sneering, Malloban spat on the grass again.

"What then, I suppose people try to thresh the paddy with a goat and then go around talking about that same goat?"

Malloban stopped in his tracks. "Where is it you want to go?"

"This time I'm leaving the zoo," said Utpala.

"I'm not talking about that. You want to play the cowherd so you can eat the paddy, instead of the goat. You want to go sit on a throne like those girls—"

"Who doesn't want to get herself a throne and sit on it. But it's not up to the shamkol to give me one. Monu, come here. No one can foist the job on anyone else. The hornbill will keep sitting there flaunting his beak—waiting for the Marwari trader to come and take his oil—the parakeet will fly off to her own throne. Monu!"

Avoiding the exit gate of the zoo, Malloban started walking along another path. Utpala didn't notice. After walking for a long time, she said, "What is this, it's like this maze never runs out—"

"You want to go out?"

"Where did Monu go?"

"Come on, let's walk around a bit."

"You walk around."

"What are you going to do?"

"I can't go out by myself, can I." Utpala went and sat down on a nearby bench and closed her eyes!

"Are your feet hurting?"

An empty bench—Utpala had plunked herself down on one edge of it, without touching the back—one hand on her chest—another on her lap, she was lying there pathetically like a cold wet mollusk or parasite when the sea has slipped away, pulled back by the ebb tide. Gazing briefly here and there at the tops of tall trees, the clouds and light of the sky, deliberating on who knows what kind of seemingly ultimate meaning and finding calm and stillness in it, Utpala let herself go completely; leaning over a little, she rested her head on her right hand; her eyes closed.

Monu too has fallen asleep on the grass.

SIX

The next day Utpala proposed, "Let's go to the movies."

He was off work that day too. They went to the three o'clock show. When they got off the tram, Utpala said, "We'll sit in a box, won't we?"

"No, that's a lot of money."

"Then where do you want to sit? It's no fun watching a movie if you don't sit in a box."

"Why not, it's perfectly comfortable in the lower seats too."

"I'm not talking about the comfort—"

"Then?"

"If we sit in a box, the people below will bend their necks like geese and ganders to stare at us; it'll be amusing."

Malloban laughed and said, "Oh, is that it? It's only two or three hours after all. When the audience breaks up, no one bothers to think twice about the people in the boxes."

"Of course, they do. If some familiar person sees us from below, then he'll go around telling any and everybody. It'll be great fun! Not bad, eh, the word will get around, run all over on four hands and feet—"

What an innocent, mischievous, girlish laugh—like a precocious schoolgirl—enfolded Utpala's splendid, cream-smeared, powdered face. Heehee, she kept laughing away.

Malloban sent a sidelong glance at Utpala and said, "No, that's not true—anyway, what will we get out of that?"

"It'll be great fun."

"What's the value of that kind of fun?"

"Doesn't it have any value? Just because you said so? It certainly has. It can't not have any."

Walking, Utpala said, "That day you sold the gold watch, you got three hundred seventy-five rupees—and still you're so scared to buy a box ticket—"

"What's the use of throwing away money for nothing?"

"For nothing?"

"Which familiar person will be sitting down there and see us in the box and be unable to sleep at night out of envy?" Malloban laughed at that, exposing his teeth a bit.

Utpala said, "There you told a flat-out lie."

"Why, what did I say that was a lie?"

"Did I say anything about envy?"

"It'll be such fun, it'll be such a thing to strut about—that's what you said. That may be so, but if other people don't burn with envy, how will our fun come to fruition?"

"Fine, then let them burn with jealousy!"

"Fine. Let them burn." Malloban went up to the ticket booth.

Of course, Malloban bought a second-class ticket—at the matinee, you got it for half-price—he didn't even have to spend three or four rupees.

"Forget it, I'm going home—" Utpala said, as if she'd gotten a shock while putting in a plug.

"Why?"

"I won't see the movie."

"You were the one who's been hurrying me along since morning to come see a movie."

"I've had enough. I won't ask to come anymore."

"But at least come now."

"You and Monu go."

"And you?"

"It's all right. You two go."

"Come on! Do grown-up people act so childish, Pala?"

"I saw what kind of ticket you bought," Utpala said with an angry shrug. "Childish? Me? You've sent my name down the drain. You've lost your precious honor buying that ticket. O ma, a third-class ticket!"

"Who told you that?" Malloban held the tickets in front of Utpala's eyes and said, "Second class—"

"Then why did they take one and a half rupees— they're supposed to take three rupees two annas for a second class—"

"We've come to see a matinee for the first time in a long time, that's why you've forgotten all the rules. This is a matinee—half-price—"

Utpala walked a step or two and said, craning her neck around, "Then you could have done first class."

"I thought about it, but then we would have gotten a seat way in the back."

"Rubbish! At the movies you can see best sitting in the back—"

"But you have weak eyesight—"

"Who, me?" Lifting her eyes as if to give him a resounding slap on the cheek, Utpala stared at Malloban.

"If I don't have weak eyesight, your pretext for buying a second-class ticket doesn't hold up, or what?"

"You think so? Last time when I took you to first class, you spent the whole time telling me you can't see anything, you're seeing fuzzy—that day you wanted to go sit up front." As he spoke Malloban turned and stared Utpala straight in the face and said, "You're just standing there—"

"I'll catch a bus at the turn on the big road and go away."

"You won't see the movie?"

Utpala kept her face turned away.

Malloban said, "Fine, let's go home then—"

"Return these tickets and get the money back."

"Why would they take them back now?"

"Then sell them to somebody."

"Who will buy them?"

"True, no one will buy them if they see that rag around your neck and that bristly beard."

Of course, today before going out Malloban had put on a silk panjabi—and he'd shaved too.

Stiffening, laughing, teeth smeared with laughter, with hesitation and diffidence, Malloban started looking this way and that. Who could he sell the tickets to? He tried a few places but had no luck. Then one gentleman fingered the tickets and said, "Today's date, right? There's all kinds of conmen in Kolkata. Never mind, it's today's date all right. Yes, these are the center seats we wanted—me and my two girls. Fine, you'll take two annas off the price of each ticket, so you'll have to take six less than your due. All your money was going to the dump after all—"

Taking his money-bag out of his pocket, the gentleman said, "The eight-anna tickets have all run out, eh? And I've come all the way from Chetla to see a movie in Kolkata. I can't go back now—otherwise I buy all these elephant tusks and frog legs straight from the office. So here you go, take one rupee and give me all three tickets, what else."

Taking hold of Malloban's panjabi hem and giving it a tug, Utpala said, "The bell's rung inside. My feet are hurting standing here so long, and here you still haven't finished this nonsense."

At that, the three of them lifted their feet to go; the gentleman called out, "Oh moshai, oh moshai, do you hear me? I'll give you the full rupee and a half. Take it, come on, take it. Oh moshai, oh dada!"

Dada! The three of them ducked inside. Monu in the middle, the two of them on either side; on the cushioned chair in the darkness Monu was enjoying herself thoroughly—Malloban too. The "book" had begun.

Ignoring the screen, Utpala kept looking up—to see if she could determine who's sitting in the boxes, to see if her eye fell on some familiar face, to see who's sitting in the first-class seats; all this kept her busy for more than a few moments. But in the darkness, she couldn't make out much of anything. Then, letting out a sigh, she wearily turned to look at the screen. An Anglo-Indian man was sitting in the seat next to Utpala, puffing on a cigarette; it gave her a nasty feeling.

She said to Malloban, "You come here. I'll go sit in your seat."

After changing seats, Utpala saw that beside her an Anglo-Indian girl was eating chocolate and coughing—

Coughing incessantly—

Utpala felt terribly irritated, one after another four or five firingi girls had sat down. Utpala said to Malloban, "Are these five BNR girls or telephone operators—"

"Quiet."

The girls had shown up expressly to broadcast the news about their households, cooking-pots, and now and then the meaning of the film, at the top of their lungs. As they satisfied the urge to talk of domestic things, laughing, clamoring, shrieking aloud, it was they who were keeping the picture lively—

"They don't know anything, don't understand anything, what else will they do in these End Times, they just go on shouting—" Utpala said, shifting a little in her seat and letting out a sigh of mingled curiosity and melancholy.

"Who are you talking about?"

"Those firingi girls, can't you hear them fibbing?"

"Why are you harassing them?" Malloban said, putting his hand on Utpala's shoulder once, briefly.

But Utpala still had plenty to say. She said in a low voice, "We're watching the movie, bapu, and so are you. It's quite a picture, that I can see, but just for that are you going to throw rotten eggs all over and make the place into an egg stew? Someone's come onscreen wearing torn trousers—there I go hee-hee. A donkey goes running— there I go hu-hu, hu-hu. Somebody took a pair of fake mustaches out of their pocket—there I go ha-ha. A mouse jumped out of a basket and the ceiling caved in on our heads. Hatibagan's been set on fire, or the fire-engine's set off to the rescue, or the Damodar Babus of Shobhabajar have all been murdered—how did I end up with all these sluts in my lap!"

Malloban bent his neck to one side and lit himself a cigarette. He didn't turn to look at Utpala or the Anglo-Indian girls. The movie had not yet drawn him in. As he watched the movie, Malloban was surveying the shadowy, incomparable images of the charcoal-sketches and woodcuts of his interior existence—eyes closed. He really had his eyes closed . . . He wasn't sleeping, he was thinking something; as if someone somewhere was giving accompaniment—very far away. He was listening singlemindedly.

Giving Malloban a shove, Utpala said, "Are they from Reilly Brothers, or the Port Commissioner? Married, or widowed?"

Malloban, as if slowly coming out of the chloroform darkness of the operation table, rubbed his eyes and said, "Who?"

"These memsahebs here, sitting next to me?"

"Them?" Mostly woken up and wanting to wake up more, Malloban said then, "What will you do with them?"

"They're not even letting me watch the movie."

"Let them be. You say they're not letting you watch the movie! Just watch it, as long as you watch it, it's been watched."

"You said it! And can't you hear what lies they're telling? They're shaking them out of every single bone."

"About what?"

"What not?"

"Just turn them a deaf ear."

"They're pulling my ears and my whole head away—god," Utpala said, all prickly and palpitating. "They're squishing me. It hurts—ooh!"

"Look, just watch the movie—"

"This is why I told you to get a box. Ooh! Here, here—Ganesh came and crammed himself into my lap, good god—there—there it goes—I've had it—I've had it—"

"Watch the movie, watch the movie—"

Utpala came and sat in Malloban's seat.

Malloban had to go sit in his wife's seat. There was that same Anglo-Indian man next to Utpala. But the man was quiet. He shouldn't be any further inconvenience to her.

After looking at the screen for a few moments, Utpala said, "Nonsense story, isn't it?"

"It's not a good movie."

"It's not all that bad either, you seem to think. You're sneaking a look at it too, bapu."

"What can I do, I paid eight paisa—"

Monu was sleeping.

Rapping her on the head, Utpala said, "Look, watch the movie—we wasted a rupee and a half just for you. Eat up—eat a Ganga-river hilsa—if you don't want that, eat a stinky dried fish. Here, all these heifer-calves are gawping away with gnats in their ears. Eat what you want—eat what you want—" With that she rapped away at Monu until she woke up.

Rubbing her eyes, Monu looked this way and that, and finally turned to the screen like a magnet turning to a mountain; she got so wrapped up in the picture that she couldn't see anything anymore. Even when Utpala saw that, she didn't bother rapping Monu on the head anymore. Not in time—not in timelessness, not in her own soul or in someone else's heart—nevertheless, in some kind of chance uninterruptedness of all these familiar

and half-familiar things, Utpala bent her head and sank
down into the life, darkness, death, and disregard of an
incomparable otherworld.

SEVEN

Four or five days later Utpala took a card from the peon's hand and, blossoming with happiness as she read it, said, "They've sent news of Borobouthan."

Malloban was rubbing himself with mustard oil. "News again at this age—" he said and grimly resumed rubbing himself with oil.

"Of course, why not?"

"How old is Borobouthan?"

"Fifty-four."

"I didn't know such old housewives still have kids."

Slipping the card into her blouse, Utpala said, "What is it you want to say, why don't you break it down for me—"

"It's not that, I was saying—" Malloban quietly rubbed in some more oil.

"You don't have to say anything, I get it, your gut feeling—"

"No, no, I was thinking—" Malloban stopped, then suddenly took a plunge, "More kids at this age—"

"What's got into you, are you going to stand blocking the path and looking murderous before the boy even arrives?"

"Who'd listen even if I did—" Malloban said, cutting the words with his teeth and laughing.

Utpala went off to the terrace, humming—Raag Chhayanat, in honor of Borobouthan's baby—after Chhayanat, Bhimpalashi—then Bageshri—but only a line or so of each. Rubbing oil on his back, Malloban was thinking: When it came to herself, in these twelve years, Utpala must have closed the door to the fertility goddess Shashthi, since only one child had come along, and a girl at that; this the first child, this the last; if there's no boy to continue the line, so be it—that's how Utpala thinks. But when it comes to others, come the thirteenth or fourteenth, look what Behag, Bhoirobi, and kirtan tunes she's elaborating on the rooftops. What is this that Utpala is doing? Is she doing right? It's not right, certainly. It's not right at all. But still, this alone is right, settled!

Rubbing oil on his feet, Malloban felt: What do I know? If she were some other virile fellow's wife instead of mine, Utpala wouldn't have let him go without mothering eight or ten children by now, maybe.

Rubbing oil on his head and looking at the harshly sunny sky, Malloban was thinking: however much aversion she has to me, she might well have had just as much earnest desire for some other man; what would it be like then? By a streaming river, in the fresh wet greenery, a forest of betel would shoot up then, Utpala's betel forest, like blue-black snake heads in the sunshine and air—in the ceaseless wind and rain.

Singing a kirtan, Utpala came down from the terrace—
"How old is your brother now?"
"Sixty-four."

"Sixty-four!"

"What, was he just born today—"

"He's gotten quite old, then—"

"He's not a newborn, that's true—"

"Exactly, he's really old—"

"Look at him frothing at the mouth and going 'old, old,' this old child of mine," Utpala said. "Here, now tell me what you're going to send Borobouthan."

His body rubbed with oil, his feet with oil, his head with oil, Malloban was gleaming in full sunlight like a strange reptile. Staring into the sunlight on the terrace, Utpala's eyes were dazzled; one moment she was seeing the reptile standing there with his shiny scales, moving his hands, his eyes, the next moment everything was blurred—in the endless darkness of the inexhaustible sunshine, she could no longer see anyone or anything.

Malloban looked cruel enough, and yet at first sight not at all like that, but rather nice and shiny—so it may have seemed to Utpala; she couldn't quite put her finger on it. But this certainly didn't mean that Utpala was cowering in fear; and Malloban was showing up quite sharply. If that were so, it most likely wouldn't be good.

"I think if you try to give them something, they'll be embarrassed."

"Why?"

"With this kind of thing going on, they're already embarrassed—"

"When you were in your mother's belly, she lay there just benumbed with shame! No? Sissy, you still pushed your way out then, from the shameplant. Out you came. What came of that? All the people of the world went and ducked into a mousehole! Shame! Shame! Shame!"

Still talking, discharging her mental venom, Utpala took a turn around the terrace, came back and said, "Be that as it may, you'll at least have to buy her a Benarasi sari for fifty or sixty rupees. And a silver sindur box. I would have liked to give her a gold box. After all she's kept house with her husband for forty years—and even at fifty-four she's still bearing—"

"That Totapuri mango tree?" Malloban sneered a little, resisting the urge to laugh more, shifted away a little and said, "I know Borobouthan—"

"What, a Benarasi sari won't suit her?"

"I'm not saying that," Malloban said, coming back to the bowl of oil and glancing at it. "I don't think she has the slightest desire for anyone to make a big deal out of this."

In the distant sunshine, the reptile has flared up brightly. Like a bit of concrete in a bite of pudding, Utpala gives him a hard stare. The image blurs; Utpala's eyes are smarting with sunlight and bewilderment; as if her inner eye has been plucked out by another kind of fire—into sunshine.

"The truth of the matter is, you don't want to part with a penny. You think your own people are strangers. Hiding the fish in the greens and all that foolery, don't I know you?"

Utpala flung the bowl of oil on the terrace and broke it!

"Oil spilled, money will come," Malloban said laughing. "Well, dear, I'm going to take a bath."

When he came back from the office, he said, "Come on, let's go out."

"Where?"

"Let's go see what there is to buy—"

Some of the smoke cleared from Utpala's heart. "I told you, a Benarasi—"

"But I don't have the confidence to shop for those things on my own. Come with me—"

"You won't get one for less than sixty or seventy, those saris. The three hundred seventy-five I have for Mejda, you know I can't spend any of that—"

"There's no need for that—" Malloban said, mopping his face with his handkerchief.

"Then where will you get the money?"

"I've withdrawn it from the provident fund."

"How much?"

"Seventy-five."

Her face gleaming with smiles, Utpala said, "Oh lovely! You're really a good boy. Really, if not— Aha, you haven't even had your tea?"

Malloban went and sat down on a chair to wait for his tea. A few moments later Utpala came back, not with porota and tea, but all dressed and ready to go to the market.

A bit taken aback, Malloban said, "Couldn't we have our tea and then go?"

"That cook came awfully late today," Utpala said, lifting her right foot onto the chair Malloban had just vacated and brushing off with her handkerchief the Cuticura talcum powder that had fallen on her polished shoe, "I told him myself to put on the rice, that's the only reason he did it. Those porotas from this morning had gone cold—I gave them to Lona's mother. Her son has leprosy, they don't get enough to eat."

EIGHT

Utpala's sewing machine had been lying around for a long time—not neglected of course, she doesn't neglect things—but unused. Cleaning the cover of the machine, opening the cover, and keeping the inside dusted and glistening—if she doesn't have other work to do, this is a task she most lovingly performs.

One morning a little girl from the other family of tenants came to her and said, "Pala Auntie, do you have a sewing machine?"

"Who told you I'm your auntie?"

The girl stood looking shakily at Utpala—she didn't say anything.

Malloban said, "Ah, why are you asking her like that?"

"You never get even a glimpse of them," Utpala said, "Today when she comes for the sewing machine, it's Pala Auntie! Wonderful!"

The girl craned her neck this way and that, picked up the hem of her frock and started chewing it.

"Whose girl are you, eh?"

The girl gave her father's name.

"So you're that Shejoginni's girl?"

The girl said, taking her teeth off a corner of the chewed frock, "Yes." Utpala looked at Malloban and said, "All water runs down, eh. The Tap Above just runs by itself. This same Shejoginni was saying one day, does Kolkata water sell for the price of gold? I remember perfectly."

"What's the use of remembering all that?"

"No, no, why would you remember? Shejobou was rubbing balm on your wounds that day, offering me up for judgment on a copper plate—"

"Do you get blisters just touching copper?"

"I do indeed. It stings like wet nettles to hear that kind of talk. Ish!"

Looking at the girl, Utpala said, "Who are you, eh bapu? You're the tenants in the room next door; we don't eat or wear anything of yours; we don't trample your new pigeon-pea fields or try to cheat you by mixing your pigeon-pea fritters with heron droppings—and your mother—"

Malloban stopped Utpala in the middle and, giving the girl a couple of pats on the back and neck, looked at his wife and said, "You're no less, bapu! What does she know—what will you get out of harassing her?"

"But I won't give her the machine."

"That's another question."

"And that Shejoginni is cursed. She gave birth to four girls one after another. Gave birth to four girls one after another—"

The little girl was biting her frock; she started biting at it even more fearfully.

"You had a little sister the other day, didn't you, Khuki?"

"Yes."

"I know that. She deliberately didn't tell us. But she called in people from ten miles away and fed them. People can be so criminally stupid—"

When Utpala had hardly finished, Malloban said, "Khuki's still standing there. Either give her whatever you're going to, or tell her—"

"And yet we two families live side by side in one strip of a house—and still they don't have the brains of a cowherd."

"Do you ever call them in for anything either?"

"Why would I call them? They're calling out to me in musical tones with a spoonful of honey night and day—"

"One side has to start first, after all—"

"I'm supposed to call in a whole clan and feed them singlehandedly? They're the ones who should call the three of us and sweeten our mouths a bit at least. They could have invited this Monu over one day and given her a handful of jibegoja or shonpapri or something. We give their kids things; can't they even cough up a peppermint lozenge?"

"Never mind, to hell with them, now you—"

"And such a big family, such a crowd. The crows are eating, the wood-mites are eating, the ants are eating, the little devils are falling over themselves to clean every plate."

"Are you going to give her the machine or what! Give it to her."

"But they've got minds like scarecrow-pots. No rice will ever cook in that pot, it's full of sand; humans, animals, birds—all flee at the sight of it. A fine set of sooty pots they've sat themselves down with, Shejobou and them—"

"You've said enough in front of this girl—"

"I said it for her ears, so it hits them in the guts."

The girl was still standing there.

Malloban said, "Khuki, don't chew your frock anymore."

She dropped the frock from her mouth. They could see blood trickling out from her teeth.

Monu said, "Runny teeth."

"You have runny teeth," Utpala said, "Have your parents shown them to a doctor?"

"No." The girl (somehow like a baby shamkol, it seemed to Utpala) shook her head.

"No?" Utpala looked at Malloban and said, "See how she's chewing her frock! This girl's got dropsy, she's got no calcium in her body; and still she can't stop popping them out year after year. All twelve months are Kartik to them, baba!" The girl had quite unconsciously started to chew her frock again; Utpala gave the frock a sharp tug and said, "Du dhumshi, you smeared yourself with goat's blood— you slaughtered it—du—du—"

The girl was slowly walking away.

"Listen, Khuki," Utpala called out.

The girl came and stood nearby.

"Brush your teeth real good with mustard oil and salt every day, won't you?"

Wagging her head like a baby shamkol, the girl said, "Yes."

"I see you three sisters are as skinny as 'bamboo-leaf' fish, and just as ugly. How is your littlest sister for looks?"

"Very pretty."

"What's her color like?"

"Very fair."

"It's not a question of dark and fair," Utpala said, looking at the big shamkol like a parakeet nibbling on a red chili. "She's come out looking like a shrimp from Mograhat.

Her throat looks hollow like a plantain spathe. Such a sorry sight. Really, what skinny shinbone in a human belly—"

Monu let out a little gasp of laughter.

"What you call fair, Khuki, is a lack of blood in your sister's body. A milky, rosy complexion—that's something else."

The shamkol baby's head shook again, "No, my sister has blood."

"She does? And she's still white?"

"Very white."

"Then she's got jaundice."

"No, she hasn't got jaundice, she's fair. She's so pretty! Ish, my sister and jaundice?"

Utpala said, "You didn't show us your sister, eh."

"Why don't you come and see her."

"Why should I go see her now. Did she feed us? At the sadh? The day she was born, did she send us the news?"

Malloban said, flaring up a bit, "That's it! Now we're in for it. For who knows how long now you've been kicking like a grown cow trying to break a calf's neck! What's got into you?"

Staring into the girl's eyes as if sinking into them, Utpala said, "But you've shown up sure enough to get the sewing machine—you shamkol baby!"

At that he started and stared in such surprise at the girl and at Utpala, Malloban.

"The day your sister was born, why did you give four ulu?"

"It wasn't me."

"What ululations! I thought this time a prince had come."

Like a baby bird catching a couple drops of water from the clouds in a land parched by the sun, the girl fluttered up at Utpala's words.

"Whom did your mother tell you to ask for the machine?"

"You."

"What did she say?"

"She said go ask your Pala Auntie for the sewing machine and bring it to me—"

Utpala felt somewhat pleased, as if the clouds of Asharh had just dampened the dry earth of Joishtho, she fiddled with the girl's curly hair, and said, "How did I become your auntie?"

"Ma said so."

"You've got a lot of lice in your hair, Khuki."

"Yes, I got them from my older sister's hair."

"Nobody picks the lice out of your hair?"

"No."

Utpala said, squishing one louse after another to death with her thumbnail, "Here, I'm picking them off your head. It feels nice, doesn't it?"

The girl left her head in Utpala's lap and closed her eyes.

"What will your mother do with the machine?"

"Sew shirts."

"For whom?"

"Chordi, me, my little sister—all three of us."

"But your mother's still in confinement."

"No, she's come out."

"When?"

"Just three or four days ago—"

"Her pulse must still be weak! How will she sew? Her veins will start throbbing."

"She asked for it."

"We've got kheer from Lokkhikantopur—will you have some, Khuki?"

The girl wagged her head and said, "Yes." How the shamkol chick's head is shaking, like a drop of water fallen on silver, trembling as it dries in the sun.

Utpala washed her hands and gave the girl a little of the kheer. Then she carefully inspected the machine, wiped it down, and said to Monu, "Go on, Monu, give the machine to Shejo Auntie. You've had your kheer, Khuki?"

"Yes."

"How was it?"

"Great—"

"What's your name?"

"Nora. Nora, bhenge debo danter gora (Pestle, I'll break the roots of your teeth)."

"What are you studying?"

"I'm still—the letter ka—"

The little girl wiped her dirty hand on her shirt and ran off.

The baby girl next door died in confinement.

"I thought it would happen like this—"

Utpala spent two or three days overcome (or enchanted?) by a strange bereavement.

She said, "I didn't even get to see her. She didn't even call me to see her."

"What would you do if you saw her?"

"It's just next door—a person is born—dies—like the hand of a clock turning. She could have called me once at the time of death. She died the night before last at three in the morning, you said?"

"Yes."

"What was I doing then?"

"Sleeping," said Malloban. "So many children are dying."

"Did she cry a lot, Shejoginni?" Utpala remained standing there propped against the wall with stilled hands and feet, looking on this side, that side, through to the other side of the roof into a huge empty basket of sunlight.

"You sent a sari to Borobouthan—and she didn't send any news," said Malloban.

"Is it time for news yet?"

"Don't you think! It's been ten or fifteen days already."

"My brother must have written back," said Utpala, "but the letter got lost on the way."

"It's not that," Malloban said with a bit of a shrug, "Post office letters travel like an ojha's bowl. If you put a stamp on a three-paisa postcard, whatever country you send it to, it'll get there for sure."

Listen to how the big shamkol is talking, puffing up the hair on his neck—Utpala was thinking, staring at Malloban. But she didn't press the matter of the letter any further.

"They boxed up that newborn girl and took her to the cremation ground?"

"Yes."

"What kind of a box?"

"A packing box—of pine wood—"

"They trapped her inside? Hammered in nails?"

"What, you want them to wrap her around the outside of the box and stick it shut with gum and slap a label on it?"

"What did they do after that?"

"They took her to the cremation ground—"

"They don't burn little ones, do they?"

"No."

"No? They buried her then?"

"Yes."

"What happens after that?"

"After what?"

"I mean, what will happen to her underground?"

Malloban lit a cheroot and said, "Nobody thinks about those things. Something or the other will happen. If jackals don't dig her up and eat her, she'll rot—there'll be worms."

"Where are there jackals in Kolkata? She'll rot and turn into earth—"

Listening to this, Utpala didn't sit down on the chair in front of her but went and plopped right down on the floor, sat there propped against the wall with her legs spread out.

Puffing on the cheroot, Malloban was thinking: What an idiot! What idiotic questions. How many countries are being ruined, and here sits Utpala distressing herself . . . Then what? What will happen to her underground? Hoosh! But still, she's not an idiot, she's not at all an idiot; becoming the mother of a child—it hadn't been possible for her to be the mother of as many children as she'd wanted; all that dormant force is flowing out as the apparent idiocy of her discontent.

"All right, so if big girls die and you bury them, what happens after?"

"Why would they be buried? They're cremated."

"No, I'm talking about people who don't follow the custom of cremating—"

"Oh," Malloban gave Utpala a properly masculine, acute look.

"I've heard a very beautiful twenty-year-old girl, maybe twenty-one, in perfect health, suddenly died somehow. In the morning they buried her. Then everyone left for their own villages. There weren't any human beings for eight or ten miles around. Just after sunset, somebody came and dug up the earth and ran off with the corpse. Why did he take it, tell me?"

"A twenty-year-old girl?"

"Yes, she was really pretty, fully developed; even after they dug up the corpse, the body's beauty was in full bloom, and so well-nourished."

"That's why it was stolen—" Malloban said.

Utpala had woken up Malloban far too well, with every word, she'd woken up too well herself.

Malloban was not allowed to go downstairs to his room anymore tonight. This night Malloban and Utpala spent quite intimately. The whole night—the whole winter night.

NINE

Whatever Malloban might think, it would have been very hard for him to do away with the routine duties of a husband and father, and spend his life alone as a bachelor. In these twelve or fourteen years, on his rounds at the Goldighi, he's cultivated many a harvest of air; community service, efforts for the country's independence, exhortations to revolution, stirrings of unrevolutionary hearts, the nineteenth century's nocturnal seashore: literary, religious, intellectual; the twentieth century's flourishing primordial blood, sunshine, shadow, burning, sea-song—the import and intent of various other kinds of life, he has envied—his own life has often felt pithless, fruitless. But still, this steady job, wife and daughter, the three rooms on College Street—would any other success ever accrue to him in life?

When he fixes his mind on it, he understands—he's got his proper due out of life. He knows this life of his could have been a whole lot worse. Though he's sometimes been stirred by the scent of musk there at the Goldighi and though at night in his own bed on the first floor he's tossed and turned more than anywhere, even so he's understood that his own domestic life is not a musk deer, nor is it undomestic; those who have mounted the peak of domestic success and spend night and day embroiled in money, reputation, liquor, and women, do they know what they are, who they are, where they are going! They don't know. Their innermost soul is not right—the scent from below their navel is spattering them this way and that; sometimes it startles and distresses someone like Malloban by the side of the road. But Malloban knows, this navel is not his own—it's all theirs.

At one time his mother had still been alive. His mother had been a very affectionate and humorous person; but at that time, when he'd started his first job in Kolkata, those days spent with his mother in a single room in a one-story house in Shyambajar—he remembers every one of them: instinctive, intense, mild, monotonous, how dry and damp, the days of life. He used to think, a man finds his mother right in the delivery room, doesn't he—finds her every day—finds her abundantly—that's why the maternal bond weakens so soon—newness is lost. He used to think, there comes a time in a man's life when the damp attachment of his mother is so natural that it seems as readily available as light, water, air; if some unknown girl finds a place in his heart, it takes time to conceive of her innate organic integrity as quite as natural as the earth underfoot, as water from an earthen cup; even if she is near, she is far—translucent, candid, shining forth, she alights so effortlessly, like Bhanumati's sleight of hand—but still, so dark, solid, dense!

Thinking all this, Malloban's mind fell back diffidently; since he had fallen short before his mother, in reverence for her, in indifference to the woman he took a liking to on a street or ghat and scorn toward himself, he kept himself wakeful.

When Malloban had not yet married, how he had been pained at the sight of the married clerks in his own office going off for weekend trips! From the day he brought Utpala into his own room until today, whenever he'd heard any married man speak of bereavement, Malloban has seen that man as if melted into the fog-house of the past's infinitude, like a surpassingly dead thing seen in a corner of a museum—he has felt that that man has no future; imagining the desolation of that life, it seems that somehow the experience of disquiet and anguish has whetted another kind of edge in him. His own wife is alive—inwardly arranging this consolation all day long at his desk in the office, all night long under the covers in the downstairs room, in completely silent peace, one after another he has given them his farewells—has accepted theirs.

All this is about the foundation of Malloban's life, about a blueprint. He can't live alone, so he lives with his mother; but still, in the course of time, his mother's love and proximity seem to him to be included in living alone; he can't go on without getting married; he doesn't have the strength to get rid of his wife and go on alone.

But when it comes to the niceties of life, he's well aware of this domestic life's various shortcomings. It's filling up with the remnants of ruined crops, with the stench of rotten meat and bones. Utpala's not-just-indifference, quite possibly unlove—day after day, it's becoming more transparent. The way it can be seen now, in unfathomable transparency, it seems she never had any love or fondness for him. If she didn't, she didn't. Fondness for others? Love for another? That may well be. And still, he'll have to drag Utpala around with him until his dying day? Utpala will do the same for him, it seems? Seeing Utpala clearly, before his eyes, become attached to others—it seems Malloban will have to protect himself by physically withdrawing from that place? What in the blink of an eye has gulped down the stars of the sky, the sands of the netherworld, the false grandeur of human life, having perceived *that*, like a gowned Chinese or Greek philosopher, will he have to steady himself again— and then will he, when it's getting late, have to sit at the table and casually chat with his wife, with his daughter?

Those days before marriage, late fall before winter, early fall before late fall, the surpassingly transient possibility of fall in the fields, in the sunshine, in the faces of people, in the chatter of birds, the magnanimous magic in the imminent winter night, just so they seemed to him—

Could he go away again to the land of that world before marriage? As soon as he posed the question, he got the answer: a man keeps moving on toward death, he can never turn back. Still, it's highly possible to deduct Utpala and Monu and proceed toward death—alone. In his mother's time he couldn't, but his wife has set him on his feet: he can go on walking consciously through the darkness—to unconscious death. He can.

But all these desires, these thoughts, are temporary. It's not that in Malloban's mind, there's no earth–circling rebel or thinker; there are devils, swindlers, and inhuman people in him too, but above all the man has remained true to himself; an ordinary, god-fearing, and fearful man. If he'd found an ordinary, affectionate, god-fearing, and fearful wife, then these two straightforward lives could have come to an end one day peacefully, without contributing any special fruitfulness or fruitlessness to the world. But that didn't happen. No, the house did not fill up with humble, tame tenderness; it crackled like a fantastic fire-witch of straw—Malloban's marriage, wife, and married life.

Utpala is very good-looking; it's not enough to say very—very! Healthy. The keenness of her taste and intelligence sometimes makes itself very clear; even the hostility and hardness of her heart melts like wax in some places, in the heat of some people, or in the touch of willful sin, then cools and hardens like wax again when she returns to the domestic environment. As a prospective bride, this girl was very valuable—as a woman also. But it wasn't right for her to become the wife of a man like Malloban. Utpala is hardly lacking in friends and relations. Plenty of people from her father's hometown know her—love her—come to see her; it's through them that she's become acquainted with many more people in Kolkata; within ten or fifteen minutes with Ut, Pala, Utpala, etc., a hundred kinds of people feel the need to say a hundred kinds of things; this whole mixed crowd used to come around a lot; their coming and going has ebbed a bit now, it seems; it also seems it will be on the rise again soon. Those who come and go in this house—some stay fifteen minutes, some two or three hours. Almost all of them go straight to Utpala on the second floor; Malloban is sitting in the downstairs room, reading the newspaper, puffing a cheroot; whether they see him or not, they feel they've seen everything, feel amused or bored or callous. But nobody feels much need to enter into a detailed discussion with Malloban. A few of them also know that this person's wife doesn't care about him at all. After this kind of realization, a shankhini, a woman of the third classical type, not far away on the tip of time's, of the world's nipple, seems a whole lot more succulent— advancing toward her with the daring and desire of a timid, palpitating breast. Malloban has seen, known, felt all this. He has seen people familiar and half-familiar to him mounting the stairs with unblinking skill—with such urgency—such haste! That he himself, a living being, is down there in that room—that even this house is his, that's nothing—and the thing is, that's perfectly correct.

None of those who go upstairs come down shamefaced, do they? Some of them sit around for a long time; laughter, mockery, raunchy jokes, outrages come spattering down in foaming drops into the room downstairs; Malloban sometimes thinks, taken aback—thinks things. A nest of smoke-black birds of thinking things, this head of his. Suddenly lighting a cigarette or slamming open the shutters, he drives off the birds. He never follows those who go upstairs; he never goes and says anything to them. Even when the gathering has gotten lively in the room on the second floor, somehow he still feels hesitant to go upstairs; when it's late at night and there are few people in Utpala's room—one or two—quite possibly one—then he doesn't go upstairs at all; what he's discovered with his mind, he doesn't want to discover with his eyes—the dregs of everyone's life.

He takes a bath in the tank, gets his rice from the cook, gulps it down, and goes off to the office. Or when people gather upstairs in the evening, he takes his stick in hand and slowly goes off to the Goldighi. He walks and thinks: How many more days? I'm circling this square—in the blink of an eye, twenty years will whiz by over my head, over Utpala's; our hair will turn gray before our eyes, our teeth will fall out, and then nothing but moaning wind will remain. Even as he thought, look, he's really crossed the distance of twenty years—this life is now quite solitary, silent; there's not an extra crow, an uninvited cat anywhere; in the sunlight, in the air, unconcern is spread out in all directions; as much as you want! How much will you take? As if even as he thinks, in the force of forgiveness, the sap of the wet month of Shrabon drips into every vein of the dry earth of Boishakh and Joishtho. Malloban lights a cheroot.

They've made it across twenty years, he and Utpala. All the cycles of excess that have occurred in the last twenty years in Utpala's life—he doesn't have time to think of them anymore. In the night at the Goldighi, in the winter, in Malloban's mind, his cheroot brings down some kind of silence, certainty, peace, like the glint of Shanto's mother's fire in that winter night of childhood. Walking home, coming close to the house, Malloban was saying, to who knows whom: "My dear, all the knaves have gone away—even the knave of hearts—tell me. Twenty years slipped away before we could even blink. Monu's at her in-laws' house, and the lord and lady are upstairs in our house—tell me! The bed is nice and warm and cosy for two people, is there no end to the winter night, tell me!" In the middle of the night, across the cold river, the head of a shamkol seemed to be rising and falling like a dhenki, as Malloban was saying, "Tell me, tell me!" Still saying, and shivering, Malloban ducked into his room and pulled the covers around him; in the midst of so much darkness and so much sleep, there's no longer any such thing as a human body, even the mind goes wooden, and if you wake up suddenly the wood catches fire; waking up suddenly all through the night and burning; Malloban woke up in the morning in another kind of fire, of waking consciousness. Here that snarky shamkol's "tell me, tell me" cleverness won't fly; counting every second and minute, rejecting the metaphor of the fire-chameleon as false, accepting fire as real fire, he would have to go on step by step. There's no other method, there's no other way anymore.

One day Malloban heard at the office that the wife of the office clerk Manmohan Babu was terribly ill—she'd been taken to the medical college hospital.

"Don't worry, Manmohan da, she'll pull through—" said Malloban.

But that whole day at the office he felt disturbed, his mind kept straying toward Utpala.

In the evening, when he went home, he headed upstairs without even changing his clothes. When he got there, he saw that Utpala and Monu were sitting on the terrace—who's sick, where?

"You're feeling alright, aren't you, Utpala? Our Manmohan Babu at the office, his wife is awfully sick—"

"What sickness, Baba?" Monu asked.

"Oh, it's some kind of sickness, she's got a stone—"

"What's that?"

"What do I know."

For a few moments Malloban stared outside with eyes of light and shadow and grew very pensive; letting out a sigh, he said, "Monu, what we eat has all kinds of things in it. When they don't get digested, a stone forms inside—"

"Is it in the stomach, the stone?"

"No, not in the stomach, it can be in the kidney—or in the gallbladder—"

"What's a kidney, what's a gallbladder—?" Malloban cut off the questions with a sweep of the hand and said, "You don't need to know all that—"

"All those stones in the rice, they build up in the kidney, is that it?" Monu said.

"No, it's not that. Not quite—"

"I could have one in my stomach too—" Utpala said.

"No, how could that be, Utpala—" Malloban said, waving away this childish ghost story with a little laugh.

"Couldn't it? That Thakur of yours is sure conscientious when it comes to cleaning and cooking the rice," Utpala said. "Some days when I sit down to eat, I see a heap of grit and stones. My stomach flips over with every mouthful, if a stone doesn't come out of that then I don't know what will—"

"That doesn't cause stones—that—" In any case, Malloban called the cook.

"Why is there always grit in the rice?"

Seeing Thakur about to object, Malloban said, "If I ever see grit, stones, or bits of rock again, I'll cut off your wages and kick you out. You'd better watch it!"

When Thakur went away, Utpala said, "What's the use of scolding him. It's the bosses who pass off adulterated rice. I'll sift the cooked rice out of their bellies in our sieve and turn it back into raw rice; go on, bring me a few bags of that belly rice. Can you do it? You just gave Thakur a thrashing out of nowhere. Idiot!"

"This time, I'll take the rice man to task," Malloban said with a yawn, still dressed head to foot for the office.

The earnest concern that had brought him home to Utpala seemed to be slowly dissolving into smoke. Since Manmohan's wife had fallen sick, all day, in the midst of all the office work, a misgiving about Utpala had been growing in his mind; in these few moments of bickering with his wife, that sad, good thing was utterly spoiled. Bad—it was all gone terribly bad. It would have been better if he hadn't taken leave from the office so abruptly and come home to this.

"She got a stone—then what—did she die?"

"No, why should she die? And if she did, how would the poor man get along?"

"What poor man?"

"Manmohan-da."

"Manmohan Babu is a clerk at your office?"

"Yes, a junior clerk. He makes fifty-five rupees; he's got a problem on his hands, Manmohan-da."

"You mean Manmohan Babu's wife's got good luck—"

"Why?"

"She's heading for the ferry—she'll go straight to heaven—she's not sticking around on a clerk's wages any more—"

Utpala said, huffing and puffing, "I feel like something's wrong in my stomach—"

"What's wrong?"

"I think I have a tumor—"

"Who said so?"

"Who's to say anything? I can feel it. How do they treat this? Will they have to do an operation?"

Malloban looked at his wife suspiciously: is she telling the truth? How can he assume it wasn't true? The situation did not seem favorable to him. Without coming to any conclusion, just because he had to say something or the other, Malloban said, "That's not a tumor. That's nothing. It's just your mind playing tricks on you."

Utpala didn't waste any more words. She was sitting on the floor—sitting there, she started to huff and puff; she got up and started to huff and puff—standing.

TEN

Four or five days went by. Malloban somehow—who knows why—didn't feel good about anything.

"Come on, let's go out for a while today—"

"Where?"

"Come on, let's go to the Esplanade for a while—" Malloban said.

"Forget it."

"Come on, it'll be depressing to sit here on the terrace alone all evening."

Utpala stood up suddenly, shaking and swinging like a blooming babla tree jostled by a strong wind, and said, "Oh, Chirongothakurpo, looks like you brought a violin—"

Her so-called younger brother-in-law Shrirongo said, "Yes, I've been studying for quite some time—Well, see for yourself how I play—"

"I can sing a few kirtans, that's all—what do I know about the violin."

"Fine, I'll play a kirtan tune."

"Sit down on the couch, thakurpo. Ah, why are you still standing?"

"I'm most comfortable standing. Nabani Mallik plays the violin standing up. My teacher."

"Nabani? Is that a man or a woman?" asked Malloban.

"If Abani's a man, then what will Nabani be?" Sending a sidelong glance at Malloban, Shrirongo turned on Utpala an accomplished, successful gaze like a charged battery.

"Abani and Nabani, two brothers? Is Nabani Babu your older brother?" Malloban said.

"I'm not a Mallik."

"Then?"

"Pala boudi knows all about my lineage—"

"They're Dottos from Rambagan," said Utpala.

Utpala asked Shrirongo, "Is this girl Nabani from the Mallik household, Rajen Mallik's—"

"Some Mallik or other. She's no boy, Nabani! She's a girl, all right. Pala boudi, should I play now?" Shrirongo asked, tilting his neck to one side like some amiable yellow bird in a forest hung with rose apples and sour star fruit.

"Play, play."

"A kirtan tune?"

"Play."

"No, not a kirtan—" Utpala quickly corrected herself.

"Why?"

"It won't sound good on violin. Play another tune, Shrirongothakurpo. What they call a violin tune—"

Shrirongo was standing with the violin on his shoulder, like a true artist. This time he shifted his weight to one foot—propping the left foot against the wall behind him, "What do you mean by a violin tune?"

"Did you know Manmohan, the violinist?" Utpala said.

"No. Where's he from?"

"The 24 Parganas. I always used to tell him to play this one splendid tune. It wasn't the tune of any song. It was a violin tune. Manmohan Mantri was the man's name."

"He only played that one tune?"

"Only one."

"Every time?"

"Twelve months of the year. He used to come to our country house when the cold hit. He'd spend the month of Kartik with us. The name I told you, does it ring a bell?"

A snail, or what was that going along—craning his neck like a goose to look at it, Shrirongo straightened up his neck again and said, "I remember, Manmohan Mantri. Now should I play?"

"Play. Play. Come here, Monu, come here. Nabani Mallik is from Rajen Mallik's household, isn't she?"

"No."

"Then?"

"Their house was in Jolpaiguri or someplace. Now they live in Kolkata. She's Keshto Mallik's daughter, from Tollygunge."

"A grown-up girl?"

"Older than Monu, younger than you, a fine mature girl. Very pretty. Her skin drips with oil like a makal fruit, beautiful but tasteless. If you stroke her, it's like dew coming out on the grass in the early morning. Plays well. Her singing is fatal, o ma. I call her my singing wife—"

"You've married her?"

"No. I just say it as a joke."

Shrirongo said, "A violin artiste doesn't marry anybody. Of course, if he found someone like you, he would, or wouldn't—she'd teach me how many Saturdays, Tuesdays there are in a year—but I've never found anyone anywhere—never seen anyone like you."

Listening to this sort of thing, even though she was past the age of blushing, the blood of that age still in Utpala's veins came sloshing up.

"Mathkotha, Nebutola, Shobhabajar, Pathureghat, Kumartuli, Ahiritola, Boubajar, Chitpur, Hatibagan, Rajabajar, Dhormotola—all of Kolkata is under my feet, Pala boudi—but I never saw anyone eat an elephant like you."

Utpala took a step back in surprise and said, "Eating an elephant?"

"Yes, like the merchant Shrimanta saw once, out in that distant sea—"

Utpala said in a mild agitation, "I suppose you're the merchant Shrimanta?"

Drawing the bow across the strings of the violin once, Shrirongo lifted his eyes to Utpala's and said, "And you're standing on the path, but why are you eating an elephant, tell me, kamini, flower of women—"

"Say Komole-kamini," Utpala said, spicing things up. "Not kamini. Don't you see they're all standing there—"

She came forward a little and said this to Shrirongo in a low voice.

This time Shrirongo began to play a single tune on the violin—very wholeheartedly, but as if wanting to fix himself on some other object of thought, in some even more attentive arrangement; Utpala understood; Malloban felt it, standing at a little distance. But suddenly, in the middle of playing, Shrirongo stopped.

"A very distant sea; one can see empty water, sunlight. There she stands on a lotus—the merchant Shrimanta sees her." Almost closing his eyes, then opening them and looking intently, slightly excited, Shrirongo said, "But why are you eating an elephant, Pala?"

"What should I eat, then?" Looking at Shrirongo, not bothering to notice Malloban standing there, Utpala let herself go quite a bit.

Shrirongo suddenly gave the room a sweeping glance and said, "Oh, here's Malloban Babu! I see he's standing here. I didn't notice. All right, I'll play a really splendid gat. Listen Monu, listen Monu's Ma, listen Malloban Babu."

ELEVEN

At two in the morning, in a house very close by, a loud sound of crying burst out, breaking into Malloban's sleep. Quickly getting out of bed and wrapping the blanket around himself, he opened the door and went down into the street. He saw a crowd gathered by the front door of Dhiren Babu's house. He went in and saw that they had brought down a girl's corpse—the girl might have been twenty-five or twenty-six, with such a pretty, peaceful, lonely face—her brow and hair smeared with sindur—at the sight, he started feeling strange inside! In the dark and cold he crept quietly back to his room; he sat on his bed for a little while, tired out; then, taking one step at a time, he slowly went up and stood in the upstairs room.

Malloban saw that Utpala and Monu were sitting up in bed. He sat down in a chair and said, "I thought you'd be awake—"

"Who's crying?"

"That Dhiren Babu's house—"

"What happened?"

"Satyen's wife died."

"What did she die of?"

"I don't know."

"Strange, we had no idea."

"She died suddenly, maybe—I hadn't heard that she had any illness."

"Heart failure. But her husband is what they call a man. Nowhere have I seen a girl draw in a son-in-law like that, by the gamcha around his neck—and I've seen my share of sons-in-law being blessed on Jamai Shasthi—" Utpala said.

"Is Jamai Shasthi over this year, Ma? What month is Jamai Shasthi in?"

Shoving Monu away with her elbow, Utpala said, "He took good care of his wife—a fair-weather dove, and on top of that, a petted one. Why did the girl faint so suddenly?"

"Who knows what happened or why," Malloban said curtly like a man soaping up his whole face in the bath.

"Aha, and there are two tiny baby girls. What will become of them?"

"Everyone will look after them. They've got a father like him. They've got a grandma, aunts, and everything," Malloban croaked as if taking care not to get soap in his eyes—while taking a bath—so it seemed.

"So one of the neighbors died, shouldn't we go?"

"I went."

"You went like a thief and came back again?"

"I couldn't stay long there, leaving you two here alone like this."

"Aha-ha, we've flown off like silk-cotton and gotten stuck on a coral-tree thorn. A hornbill will come and kindly brush us off with his bill—" said Utpala, grinding her teeth and beating the exasperation out of her body like dust out of a carpet.

"Aha-ha!—Aha-ha!" Utpala kept saying.

Getting out of bed, taking down a coarse woolen wrap from the clothes-rack, and wrapping it extremely tight around her body, Utpala said, "Come on, Monu, put your coat on."

She set off with Monu toward Dhiren Babu's house.

She's observing the formalities, fine, Malloban was thinking; but she's taking Monu with her? Why? She's not going strictly to uphold social norms—she's going to see a thing or two; food for Utpala's soul, and plenty of activity in the outside world (even at two in the morning)—Utpala will get a few hours' sustenance. Malloban lit a beedi in the darkness. But throwing it away immediately, he went down, locked the front door, caught up with Utpala on her way to Dhiren Babu's house, and said, "Here, take the key."

"What am I going to do with the key?"

"Take it. I'm going to the cremation ground."

Utpala said, wetting her lips, "As if there's no Brahmin handy, this one jumps in to burn the corpse so he can get his flattened rice—"

"Here, take the key, take it—" Malloban said, foisting the key on her.

"You'll go to some cremation ground someday, that you will. Here, get out of the way—get out of the way. There's no need for you to heave yourself up to Rama's house, wrapped in a checkered blanket, like a great wooly sheat-fish—"

"Kota shono, kota! Listen to you!" Malloban said, dropping his "h" in his heightened mental state. "Are there ever wooly sheat-fish, after all. Kota shono! Kota!" He went ahead, shivering uncontrollably—like the son of a hero's mother, going to war with the country's enemies; how else would he impress Utpala?

Some powerful stroke of childish heroism had waylaid him; as to what need there was to impress, he didn't think that far; that, in the winter night, the bed and blanket of the downstairs room were a great deal more clean, real, peaceful—in the world of value determination, this was forgotten.

TWELVE

At two in the afternoon, when Malloban came home after burning the corpse, Utpala said, "You skipped work today, then?"

"What else can I do, if a neighbor dies?"

"What did you do in the cremation ground?"

"Let me go take a bath in the tank—" Malloban said and started rubbing his back with a gamcha as he stood there.

"Did Satyen Babu go to the cremation ground?"

"O ma, how could he not!"

"O ma, you roll your eyes! I'm just asking. How long was he there?"

"He cut out at some point. I didn't notice."

"'Cut out,' what a phrase! They all had to grab him and drag him out of the cremation ground, I heard. He was all weak and worried like a trapped elephant. Did he cry a lot?"

"Yes, he cried all right. A few bucketfuls."

"The gentleman's been hit hard," Utpala said. "But he's a man after all. He'll shoo away the gadflies with his tail and start eating plantain trees again. It's about that time.

The jungle elephant will be a tame one now, and pretty soon they'll put out the plaintain leaves for twice-married Satyen's second wife's wedding feast."

"This wife is from your father's hometown, I take it? You'd like to be a bridesmaid and preside over the whole event," said Malloban laughing and twitching his body and face (as if all the teeth had fallen out of it). "What are you going to do with plantain leaves at Satyen's wedding. Satyen will be an elephant and eat plantain trees, you were saying. You'll be a kamini then, and eat that very elephant. Aha! Look at Utpala standing on a lotus like a kamini!"

Utpala had stood up. Stretching herself, she said, "You're sharp as a tack, whatever anyone says, this late in the evening. Here, go take a bath and come have your tea."

A woman's corpse—very young—has just been burnt in the cremation ground. A husband's grief still circles his wife, still deep. But already everything is thinning; solvent, successful time, pain, patter, wittiness, mischief, fear, blood, lust, in unprotected darkness and depth, there is no death, there is no void, there is no individual life, there is inexhaustible ineffable time—only time.

THIRTEEN

Since Rama died, at night now and then, Malloban began to have dreams of death and burning. One day he dreamt: he has died, he's been taken to the cremation ground; there he is quite amiably talking with everyone, greeting everyone, taking his leave, saying, I won't be seeing you anymore, who knows where I'm going.

When he woke up, he felt, how strange! A dream it may be, but in the dream, he had died; how can a dead man sit and talk with living men! Really, a dream is such a meaningless scrawl—it utterly puts to shame a man's intelligence, judgement, consciousness. Many people say that dreams come true. Is he really going to die? In the deep winter night, in the flow of ink-black darkening the darkness—thinking, thinking, thinking, he ended up like a wet mop. Not so much for himself—but if he died, what would become of Utpala? His heart started wheezing and whining, like a much older man, for Monu and Utpala. He sat up in bed; putting on his slippers and wrapping himself in the blanket, he slowly went upstairs. There he saw Utpala sleeping—beside her Monu—also sleeping. So peaceful and free of complaint, their breath. They at least haven't had any bad dreams. Great. It's heartening to look at them. But, still, if this one's husband and that one's father dies, will the two of them be able to sleep like this anymore? Even when they've woken up, they won't be able to get up, won't be able to walk around in wakefulness so easily, effectively.

But, still, ultimately, he hasn't really died. He's perfectly alive and well. He is. The name of the river of our lives—uncrossing, Malloban was thinking: nowhere can anyone cross over, never, anywhere in the course of this river; but, still, so many people traverse it every day on the strength of pain, danger, failure, death; Utpala, Monu—why won't they be able to do it? Those born human have to suffer all sorts of unpreventable blows— they have to; Monu, Utpala won't be spared; if Malloban dies, his wife and child will have to come to terms with their lot as humans; but not for very long; everything goes quiet, there's a quieted stillness. First Malloban's death— then many days later, maybe, the deaths of his wife and child; in this trinity of death, everything will go silent. Malloban's responsibility to time will run out. Everything seemed to be running out right now, as he thought—this feeling closed in on Malloban.

But another day's dream gave him more pain than ever. He dreamt: Utpala has died. In the dream, Utpala seems to be Satyen Babu's wife—the whole world knows it—Malloban knows very well himself that they've been lawfully married for ten or twelve years; there's not even a wisp of misgiving about this relationship of theirs in his mind. But, still, at the same time, in that same dream, Utpala is only wife to Malloban—nothing to anyone else; all these disjointed things in the dream seem very true and natural.

He sees that Utpala has died and is lying there stiff—her hair all messy, forehead smudged with sindur, her body—strange!—wrapped in a widow's cloth. Lying on a corpse's cot, in the various modest uncontrollable convulsions of a dead woman's mind and muscle, she is making the pain of her own death known to Satyen, but desolation, lamentation are piercing Malloban alone, to the quick.

His sleep broke.

The end of the night.

Under the blanket, his entire body is covered in sweat. He got up quickly and went upstairs barefoot. There he saw Monu sitting up in bed—Utpala's not there. That she's not there, won't be there, his dream has told him. It seems this non-existence is tied to that. She's not there.

"Where's your mother, Monu?"

"She went to the bathroom."

She's there, then; or maybe she's not; what meaning is there in such a cold night shrouded in emptiness, in the distant darkness of the bathroom, of human existence, of the statement "She went to the bathroom" that emerged from Monu's mouth?

"When did she go?"

"Just now."

"She was lying in bed asleep all this time?"

"Yes."

"She's not sick or anything, is she?"

"Who? Ma?" Monu shook her head and said, "No."

"Any discomfort? Was she crying?"

Pushing a handful of hair out of her eyes, Monu said, "No. I saw her, she didn't cry. Who told her to—did you tell her to cry?"

"Oh no." Malloban had spoken standing, now he sat down in a chair.

Malloban told his mind, just escaped from the dream and eager for reason: what is this fit of grief, of tears, wincing, wrenching in front of Satyen Babu, in thigh-quivering wretchedness—since she's died herself? Really, a dream is such a sly thing—a dense thing; those who think that if you gorge yourself and get indigestion, you dream all those scraps of dreams, do they know anything? A dream is a terminal thing—there's nothing after it; in the warp and woof of lesser and greater darkness, in the light of the night, if the end draws near, then dreams are dreamt—bad dreams; good dreams too, astonishingly sweet dreams, all of them—

"What time is it, Baba? It's morning, isn't it?"

"No. Are you going back to sleep? Go to sleep, go to sleep."

"The garbage carts are creaking. Those are the garbage carts, aren't they? The crows are calling. What time of the night is it, Baba?"

"What time of the night? I'll tell you," Malloban said. But he didn't feel like sitting down with the first section of the arithmetic book. Immeasurable inexpendable dream-heap—his mind was deep in thought about that knot of knowing-unknowing—within the fringes of the more immense knot of Utpala. To transcend all knots and reach the height of normality—

Utpala came back from the bathroom and said, "You're sitting here—"

"Are you going to sleep now?"

"What are you up to?"

"No, nothing. I thought, did you come down with something?"

"Who? Me?"

"You slept well all night?"

Looking Malloban up and down, Utpala said, "What are you here for now?"

"I just came. You read a lot at night, I take it?"

"I work a lot—"

"You think I've come to ask you for a timesheet. No, that's not it, I just came to talk."

"I don't have time now," Utpala said. "Go downstairs like a decent man and sleep."

"I guess you'll get in another round of sleep now."

"I'll be late getting up today. Make your own tea."

"I will. I can drink it at a shop, too. You slept well tonight? I was having such strange dreams all night."

Utpala had gotten under the covers; at the end of the night, just before she got up to go to the bathroom, another wave of sleep and stupor had surprised her; the spell, even now, had not yet broken; but the man comes up from below at just this time to cancel it out!

"Go away."

"Tonight, I dreamt you had died."

"Will you go downstairs?"

"I'll go downstairs sure enough," Malloban said, wrapping the blanket tightly around him. "I'll have to go down. But I was dreaming such hideous dreams all night. A night in the winter month of Poush, they call it Poshla in the village—all covered in fog. Freud called dreams the froth of Poshla. But what does Freud know about dreams? All those epileptics used to come to him in Vienna . . . just by making them hot boiled coffee, theories of human life won't emerge."

Monu said, "Ma's dead, that's what you dreamt tonight?"

"I dreamt that your Baba's riding on a backward donkey with a gift—he's going to give it to Brahmamohan Babu of Bajeshibpur. He's going—going—there's no end to his going—where is he going on that backward donkey? To Bajeshibpur's Nakori Khoshal Botbyal—"

Monu flashed a smile and said, "Bhomba! Bajeshibpur—Ba-je-shi-bo no-kori kho-sha-l—"

Lighting a beedi in the darkness, Malloban cracked his lips in a laugh. He was enjoying himself thoroughly; darkness on all sides—maybe thinning a bit; the room still full of good quiet remnants of darkness; quite cold; he's sitting in the cold wrapped up in a checkered blanket over warm linen. Like two birds huddled together in an egg-filled nest, his one human body felt warmed. Outside the sounds and stirrings of life have begun—and still there is plenty of the mouth's silent immortality. Inside the room, enfolded in the covers, Utpala and Monu are sleeping very comfortably; Pala hasn't died, Monu is alive and well; from what Pala said about going to Bajeshibpur on a backwards donkey, it's clear—this much is clear, that she's calm and coolheaded. Fine, they're fine. There's still a little left of the night to get through. Let them sleep. Malloban thought of getting up. The beedi had burnt out. He would go down now and light a cheroot, sit for a while.

FOURTEEN

The next evening Malloban came home from the office, had his tea, and came upstairs.

"Who did you give those porotas to the other day?"

"What day?"

"That day I went to buy a Benarasi for Bouthan?"

"Oh, I gave them to Lona's mother."

"Has Lona's mother come since then?"

"No."

"What was it that happened to her son?"

"Leprosy."

Utpala said, "Why are you asking?"

"A leper—that's why I'm thinking—"

"I told Lona's Ma to come every day for rice, dal, and fish."

"You did well to tell her that; people like her have to burn themselves in the stove to boil their pot of rice. A soul-searing experience—"

"But she never came back."

"A leper after all, who knows what happened—"

"No, nothing happened to the old lady," Utpala said.

"I'm talking about the son—"

"That's true, maybe he's gone to some ashram."

"That could be!"

Not much—a little—agitation seemed to have come over Malloban. Fluttering his eyelids a few times in quick succession, he said, "That day you kept me fasting and gave the porota to Lona's Ma—"

"She asked, why shouldn't I give them to her?"

"You did the right thing to give them to her. You did well. You did well—"

Malloban thought he wouldn't take the matter any further. He hadn't come primarily to talk about the other day's porota. He had an urge to talk over many other special intimate things; but still he said, "You gave them to her, you did well. But you could have given me something too, I come home after working the whole day—"

He's come to wag his tongue about what porota from who knows when—Utpala said, her voice growing heated, "You could have ordered food from outside—"

"In the future, I'll have to do just that. Otherwise, I'll be the loser. But I was telling you—"

"I don't feel any need to listen."

Malloban said a bit severely, "Why not, you've got two ears, one on each side of your head."

Even more severely, Malloban's wife said, "My ears are not for listening to any and everybody's nonsense."

Malloban felt this conversation with his wife had gone awry. Making as if to laugh it off, he said, "What I want to say doesn't get said. I end up saying all sorts of other things. I'm incapable of expressing myself properly. Don't take it the wrong way." Utpala had picked up a comb and was combing her hair—not so she could tie it up—just for its own sake. Combing her hair, she kept quiet.

Domestic discourse came to a close for the day. Malloban went downstairs. But he hadn't meant to waste his breath talking about that afternoon's snacks; his intention had been to touch the edge of things so much more subtle and deep.

A talk finished leaves a pleasant aftertaste. A different success.

But nothing came of it.

FIFTEEN

Malloban went downstairs feeling somehow excluded from subsistence. Nothing felt good to him.

They had been speaking of his wife's interests all this time—Malloban looked around at all four corners of his own room; in fact, it's due to the utter lack of motivation on the part of the mistress of the house that this room has ended up in this wretched state—compared to the orderliness of the upstairs, this room seems topsy-turvy.

For a second, his mind contorted—why should he lie here in this room any longer? Doesn't he pay the rent on all these rooms? The whole household is run on his money. But still—

He set his mind to tidying up the room.

He put the kerosene-wood tables outside, he dusted and wiped out the wardrobe, he beat down all the soot with a broom, he cleared away the cobwebs, he swept out a number of cockroaches, (he didn't have any Fleet or DDT on hand), he squished them to death underfoot, he decided not to wait for the washerman, he would scrub the heap of dirty clothes himself, he spread a clean newspaper on the little jarul-wood table, he thought that in the afternoon he would buy a shiny black tablecloth, bring a flower vase, some flowers, a couple of smart little pictures for the walls.

The next morning, he took a quick bath, ate breakfast, and went to the office. When he came home from the office, he brought the necessary things: tablecloth, flower vase—

He spent two hours arranging the room. He looked outside and saw the night had grown dark. In this cold, no one came to use the bathing tank anymore. If he snuck down and sat there scrubbing clothes, no one would find out. By ten o'clock at night, he had almost finished scrubbing. Himangshu, Shrirongo, and a few other people had gone up to Utpala's room; a violin was playing a gat; Utpala herself was singing—she would sing more—the violin would play more—they would sing (in chorus); to Malloban, this was a relief; the later into the night the music continued, the more he stood to gain—after scrubbing the clothes and before dinner, he would get a chance to rest. He washed and wrung out the clothes, stuffed them into a couple of buckets, got his bath out of the way, parted his hair, and went and lay down on the bed. Clamping a cheroot between his teeth, he slowly began to enjoy the peace of an orderly disciplined life. But one cheroot—two cheroots burned out—he waited a long time, and still the call for dinner didn't come. He had to lie there quietly in bed even longer. Then he fell asleep. Starting up in a flutter, Malloban stayed half-sitting half-lying on the bed for a while, then sat up, and seeing Thakur enter the room, said, "Ah, they're still singing—"

"The singing's not in our house."

"Then?"

"Somewhere in the neighborhood—"

Malloban listened carefully for a moment and said, "Oh, right, it's recorded music."

The upstairs room was stone-silent, for sure. Malloban went up the steps.

Thakur said, "Didimoni and Ma have gone to sleep."

"Really? You're here very late today, Thakur. What's the matter? Didn't they eat?"

"They ate."

"When?"

"They ate with two babus—"

Malloban kept quiet for a moment and said, "There's rice for me, isn't there?"

"There is. Should I bring it to you here?"

"Don't bring too much. I feel sort of nauseous—"

He ate a few bites and got up. The maid mopped up the scraps and took away the plate. The maid and the cook went home.

Malloban was feeling terribly nauseous. He closed the door, spread out some papers, and retched for a long time, copiously.

He just kept thinking of his mother. He thought in surprise: she's in this very room—I sense her standing in this very darkness; maybe she's sitting on the edge of my bed; she's stroking my body, chest, back; maybe—

Malloban felt: Utpala too is Monu's mother—she's a mother after all; she'll grow old like Malloban's mother one day too. Mixing up this mother with his own mother, just as thin, restless rainwater mixes into the natural calm of deep, collected pond-water, he seemed to long for an ideal soul of unfailing motherhood. His own mother—who is not here today, whom Malloban has seen turning to ashes on Neemtola Ghat ten or twelve years ago—Malloban's mother's indistint gesture has not yet died—another woman has come into this room to conceive and bear; Monu's mother has become a mother. Malloban today is not exactly Monu's mother's husband; that dead mother of Malloban's and this living Utpala—hoping to find these two women as one person—as a mother—inside this room, he began to look around in a strange wide-eyed disquiet; let her come in the image of his mother, or in the guise of Utpala— he would seek out both within both of them—he would find one mother—motherhood: what Malloban would find now was her infinitude, untouched by desire, without the scent of wife. Malloban let out a few cries and called out indistinctly—to mother, to Thakur, to the maid—to Monu's mother, or to Utpala, it was hard to tell.

Slowly his fit of vomiting subsided—stopped.

Malloban looked up with a start and saw Utpala standing there.

"When Thakur was leaving, he said you were throwing up. What happened?"

"What do I know."

"What did you eat?"

"Nothing, just rice."

"Not junk from the bazaar?"

"No."

Utpala said, "Do you feel like you're going to vomit more?"

"No, I don't think so."

"Is your stomach hurting?"

"No, nothing like that."

"All right, lie down, go lie down. I'll fan you."

Malloban lay with his head on the pillow getting fanned for a few moments, then said, "I feel good now."

"Anyone who's become a mother," said Malloban, "can't help coming to the head of a person's bed. You're Monu's mother sure enough, my wife. But there's no end to time; after all, we dwell within time; the hand of time comes and wipes away this thing here—wakes up that thing there; you're a person's wife; you're a person's mother yourself, a person; in the ceaseless flow of time, your mother-form blossomed, after all; I see it. I can see how you took one or two revolutions of time and formed them into such a lovely ring of knots. Just now you came down in this bone-chilling winter night, descending the stairs. You could just as well not have come. For a long time, I didn't even hope you would come. But you came even so—"

A few fingers of Utpala's left hand caught Malloban's fancy. But those few fingers didn't make any special response. Malloban had sunk so deep in the self-forgetfulness of his own imagination and sincerity that he was in no hurry to sift through the mystery of his wife's fingers. The Soul had not given him strength and time to comprehend mystery in the harsh light of clarity; the poor man, in many senses blind and senseless, was trembling with joy like a tiny bat in an abandoned room. But Malloban has sub-imagination, even sub-genius; even if it's not very well regulated. As a result, instead of a sun of consciousness, he had found endless stars of subconsciousness. It's quite possible Malloban has a sixth sense on top of the five. What in science they call the fourth dimension, it's in that land of cleverness that he is dwelling. As a result, that divine center point of mother and motherhood had caught his eye. But he can't live very long on that summit; soon he broke off and fell down into his little world of little notions—into the eddying foam of conjugal craving, desire, and disappointment.

Utpala's hand-fan had never moved with much emotion; it had been in rapid motion a little while ago. Now it was gradually slackening.

"Sometimes I feel it would be lovely to live alone. Some people live alone; for sure, our headmaster spent his whole life that way, but in his last years he found it hard to face. He appeared before women, sure enough, but the saintly man longed passionately for women to appear before him. Lust was born. The girls meant well, they did Headmaster Moshai the service of massaging his hands and feet every day; in return, over time, he began to take every chance to massage their cheeks in secret. It created quite a scandal. No wedding, but along came a little boy, a little girl. Still, he was a model of austerity. Over Headmaster Moshai's pyre is the region's biggest monastery. Sitting on the roof of a boat, you can see that monastery from so many miles away . . ."

Malloban went on talking, the way that when a deep rainy night is free of rain for a few moments, in village gutters, tanks, and channels, water goes babbling along as if talking to itself.

As she fanned and fanned him, Utpala's hand began to hurt, but Malloban made no move to end her pain. When he gets to talking, Malloban tends to foam up, sometimes froth, he has a great capacity for making himself suffer the suffering of enjoying himself; dhet, I don't like it; sometimes, of course, it even etherizes me—like before Monu came along. But I don't like it anymore these days, dhut.

Setting the fan down by the bed, Utpala said, "You threw up, but now what's to be done about medicine?"

"You don't have to worry about that, Pala."

"Is there any medicine?"

"No."

"Then?"

"I won't need medicine. Something turned my stomach, and I threw up—that's all. If something that bad had happened, the fit wouldn't have subsided so quickly."

"You never can tell. There's no medicine. And who's going to get a doctor?"

"No, no, I'm not sick, just a little confused." Slightly agitated, Malloban tried to sit up and, in the end, said still lying down, "It's over. If I talk to you for a bit, it will all get better."

"There's no man in the house," Utpala said with a sour, insipid face. "When people come down with this and that, it's very inconvenient. Who'll call a doctor—who'll stay up all night?"

Malloban said very smoothly, in order to iron out and polish the contortion of his wife's face, "Now I've been thinking, I'll keep a clerk—odd jobs, errands—everything will get done."

"But who'll stay up tonight and—"

"Sit here, sit with me for a while, I'll fall asleep by myself."

Utpala sat there speechless and motionless, with folded arms.

A little time passed. No one is saying anything. Someone will have to do something, it seems. No one feels good about it. There is a sort of discomfort. More time passed.

"You're so quiet?"

"What do you want me to do?"

"You were fanning me—"

Utpala stood up. She lit the lamp, looked around the room, and said, "Who stuffed those two buckets with wet clothes?"

She picked up one of the buckets, dumped out all the clothes on the floor, and went off to the tank.

"Those were clean clothes, you dumped them on the floor—" Malloban stared at the clothes, spilled out on the dirty, muddy floor, trampled underfoot by Utpala. Utpala brought a bucket of water from the tank and splashed it out all over the floor; she poured out another bucketful and looked at the floor in desperation, realizing it would take another two buckets of water to clean up the vomit. Utpala's secular heart, and what was not secular, but of the depths—what drove the secular—in the middle of this winter night, all of that started throbbing far more than hands and feet.

Utpala brought the last bucket of water and poured it out in the room; then she took a soap-scrubbed dhuti of Malloban's and started to swab the place.

"Why are you mopping that up with your own hands, aha, don't bother!" Malloban said.

In a tremulous voice like the feeble whistle of a plantain-leaf flute in the hands of a novice child, he said again, "That's not right, that's not right, you put my dhuti down—I'll give you something for wiping up filth."

The plantain-leaf flute shivered to pieces and said, "Ah, Utpala, you ruined my dhuti—I just washed it this evening with Khidirpur soap."

Utpala, with her head bent, was cleaning the floor and sweeping everything into the drain in one corner—not with her hands, she was working with her foot sort of wrapped in Malloban's dhuti; she kept working and did not answer. This sort of work was not for her to do, certainly not on a winter night; she would never do this kind of work. But she's as if possessed. That's why she's come down and is doing this awful, dirty work—even if only with her feet—what normally no one would be able to make her do even by beating her. She's possessed by a ghost, a tough ghost; stupefied, Utpala kept rubbing her foot on the floor and thinking.

Staring at the muddy vomity ruin of the dhuti wrapped around Utpala's (churning-stick-like) foot, Malloban started saying something, somehow, "That nice dhuti from Karim Bhai Mill—I just bought it some fifteen days ago—and this is what you've done to it—it's not even fit to wear anymore."

But Utpala needed yet another dhuti—the one from Kalika Mill. Malloban's very marrow got a wrench. Of the many people to whom one dhuti or wrap could seem so much more valuable, so much more necessary than a month's wages—Malloban was one. As a result, he recoiled, pointedly, in a fit of grief, let out a string of little trivial utterances; but all the time, his voice was mumbling, buzzing, tingling, like a lonely bamboo-bug on a late autumn afternoon—plaintive and pathetic, without heat, without warmth.

Utpala felt like laughing—sometimes she felt pity for the man; just to see him slightly crushed she'd mopped the soiled place with two of his nice dhutis—as though, thinking this, the pleasure of tormenting him had lost some of its intensity, Utpala kicked the two cloths out of the room.

"What had to happen, happened," Malloban said, gathering great strength, great moral courage. "Don't mope about it." He spoke (it seemed to Utpala) from the cave of austerity and self-purification of a sternly and zealously regulated life.

Utpala had taken the soap from a niche in the wall and was wringing her hands—she wanted to go wash her hands, feet, neck, face.

"Where did you put those two cloths? They won't get stolen, will they?"

"The door on this side is closed. Still, the neighbors' maids and servants go up and down the stairs to the roof all night. If they see them, they might take them away."

"Take them away—? Won't you keep them inside the room?"

Without a word, Utpala went to the tank and washed her hands and feet, neck and face thoroughly and came back. Taking out a towel, just back from the washerman, out of Malloban's box, Utpala started scrupulously rubbing dry her hands and feet, face and back. Then she slipped her feet into the slippers and got ready to go upstairs.

"Come and sit by my bed, won't you?"

"No, I won't sit anymore. What's this, I've put on your slippers. Where did my shoes get to? Ish, the mosquitoes are biting! Never mind, I'm off—" Utpala said.

"All right, go—get to sleep."

Like a boshontobouri bird in the small hours of the night, as he gazed at a heap of stars and darkness before falling asleep again, spilling over a bit, with a laugh, going beyond the willing-unwillingness to wake up, to stay alive, (it seemed to Malloban) someone leapt over him. Was it Utpala? Lighting a cheroot, Malloban said to himself, no, it's not Utpala; the thing Malloban has ascribed to Utpala, that bodiless soul—isn't; wasn't; still it slipped away just this moment; upwards, even farther up on the pretext of going upstairs, somewhere it merged into the open air, at the summit of the spiral staircase of the winter night, among the stars.

The next night, in the upstairs room, Malloban was saying to Utpala, "This bed of yours is nice and big."

"Yes, Baba gave it to us when we were married. He had no intention of cheating the groom's side."

"I never said that."

Utpala was neatly unfolding the bedspread, fresh from the washerman—she kept at her work without a word.

"I was thinking, two grown-up people could easily fit in this bed."

"They could, so what."

"I could sleep in this bed tonight, couldn't I?"

"Then I'll have to go down and sleep in your bed."

"Why?" said Malloban, as if looking right through Utpala to see some supremely good soul. "You'll sleep beside me."

"That's exactly what won't happen," Utpala said with calm firmness, compressing her lips, her teeth, like a competent caretaker.

"Your Mejda and Bouthan will sleep in this same bed, the two of them?"

"They find that comfortable."

Malloban said, lighting a cigarette, "And we won't?"

"You can't have something just by wanting it," Utpala said, not to Monu, but to Malloban.

"That's for sure." Malloban didn't trust himself to bring the paan in his hand to his mouth. He didn't smoke the cigarette either, but threw it out the window—the burning cigarette—

He said, "If that's how it is, then I might as well go sleep on the footpath."

Done laying out the neat bedspread, Utpala said, "You'll never sleep on the footpath. But you might as well try it someday. Go on, go try it today."

"If I sleep on the footpath, your face will brighten up."

"You're saying yourself that there's no difference between a decent person's bed and the footpath—"

"I see there isn't. Why isn't there? Why isn't there? Can you put your hand on your heart and tell me?"

"You'll be told in good time," said Utpala. "But what about sleeping on the footpath?"

"The way things stand, I don't have any strong objection to it."

Utpala hung the mosquito net, put out the light, lay down on the bed, and said, "If you have no objection, then what's stopping you?"

Striking a flint and lighting himself another cigarette, Malloban said, "I'm going to sleep—"

"Where? In your own room?"

"No—"

"On the footpath? Go—" said Utpala: as if wrapping herself in the leaves and fibers of sleep-creepers as she moved into the distance.

"Come and see, why don't you."

"I've seen it," she said and turned over; as soon as she turned over, wrapping herself up in the quilt, Utpala fell asleep.

From the sound of her breathing, Malloban sensed it: lulled into deeper comfort than a cuddly cat, the woman had fallen asleep—a strong blend of the warmth of cotton and the cold of winter was enough—there was no need for a man's touch, for Utpala—

Malloban went downstairs.

After a sleep in the midnight cold—in the warmth—his own bed didn't seem so bad. It seemed to Malloban that all day—and the first part of the night—a man's mind, like a stupid glutton, wants—waits, austerely endeavors, as if it had nothing of its own, someone else had to come and give, and then it would have. But in the depths of the night, in bed, the body alone is taste. The body alone gives everything to a man. What is the mind? Who is the mind? The mind is nothing. In a fine dense winter night, Malloban was savoring the body.

Utpala had indeed dispensed with a man's close contact; but for all that, not with the body's sensuality. In the depths of the night on the second floor in her own bed, she was savoring this strange feeling.

SIXTEEN

The arrangement of things in Malloban's room had begun to bare its teeth as before; mounds of dirty yellowed papers all around, through the window endless dust and smoke from the street, the incessantly pattering nests of pigeons, cheroot-stubs all over the floor, bruised cheroots, tobacco leaves, ash, matchsticks, bird feathers and droppings, fragments of an old discarded lantern, a pile of broken chimney glass; unending rows of dirty oil, acid, and medicine bottles, pots and pans, water jugs, a heap of sacks and baskets, eight or ten pairs of torn, flattened canvas shoes, dirty shirts, mosquito net weights—no doubt by some mysterious divine power, there is not a sound to be heard, nothing can be seen to move, but throughout the room old women, like dried fishes, like witches, like little old heaps, seem to be carrying on day and night, weeping and wailing, assaults and violations—Malloban could sense it, could feel it.

He had thrown the vase into a corner. From the moment Utpala had disapproved of this thing, it was as if some damned disharmony of design was welling up out of it—in the middle of a heap of pots and pans, the broken-brimmed vase had rolled to a halt.

One night a kitten took shelter in this same room. He had fallen asleep for the night; a mournful howl forced him awake; he sat up. He realized that someone must have dropped the kitten in through the window. When a man can't stand a thing himself, he shows such cunning—such dexterity in foisting it onto someone else, Malloban was thinking; but what could be done with the kitten? The way the kitten was crying with gaping mouth in the face of the flood of wind, it might even wake those sleeping upstairs.

It could be thrown back out onto the street through the window—and the window shut after it. What would happen to the kitten then—no need to worry his head about that. Kittens and puppies make their way in this world—or they die. The ones that are dead, they're done for; the labyrinth has been averted; they don't need direction, sympathy, shared shelter anymore; superlative peace; the pain, the glory of living is no more. But still Malloban could not content himself with giving the kitten that kind of peace.

Two in the morning—no milk, no food; nothing to give the kitten now; sitting on the bed, Malloban settled down to endure its crying for the long run. As if the mythological Malloban mountain had turned into the Mountain of Patience, and still the crying has not stopped—so endless is it. One by one, a number of thoughts were crossing Malloban's mind: he was thinking of this kitten's parents, how they're shaking out their limbs, shaking life out; before giving birth to this litter of kittens, on soot-black and moonlit nights, these two grown cats had been under a fairy-spell; what have they not done; but before giving birth to the next season's kittens, inevitably they will couple again; but now they are free of responsibility for the last season's, all the past seasons' deeds. They give life the slip this way, and still life indulges them, even in ever-new seasonal meetings—again—and again. Life would punish humans severely for this sort of behavior. Fine, but he still does not want to punish this kitten's parents.

Malloban's thoughts turned a corner, he forgot the story of the fairy-charmed couple; he said to himself, the saying "a dog's or cat's life" says it all—really, these creatures lead miserable lives. This kitten is maybe three or four months old—motherless, no sisters and brothers, of course no anxiety over its lack of patrimony, like Jabala's son—Malloban was thinking, lighting a cheroot—

But that mournful howling grew even more violent; taking a few drags on the cheroot, he was thinking: on this restless winter night, some spineless bastard slipped this thing through the window into his dark hovel.

There was indeed a time, thought Malloban, when this kind of thing would have been an outrage if it happened to a human baby, but the human world today is a madhouse—a human baby is no better off than a baby kitten.

There are no mosquitoes in the room; Malloban had hung the mosquito net for fear of rat bites; lifting the net, he leaned back on the pillow and sat there with the cheroot in his mouth.

A little later, he got up and turned on the light.

Frightened by the sound of human movement, by the light, the kitten stopped for a bit. But as soon as Malloban came back and sat on the bed, the crying began again. Such crying is altogether unlike the grumbling and rattling of trams, buses, lorries; to endure this, you must consider and comprehend creation itself, the agreement and disagreement of the Upanishads' and Einstein and Whitehead's accounts of god; you need a lot of compassion and patience. These Malloban lost, at the wrong time.

Leaping up from the bed, he ruthlessly drove the kitten away. In this jungle of a room, it hides in all kinds of impossible places—lies in wait—as soon as he went back to the bed, it promptly found the strength to start whining again, and Malloban was utterly consumed by hate.

This time, he caught the kitten.

Catching it, he flung it against the wall so hard that within a moment or two it died, moaning.

For the next five or six days, Malloban could not speak to anyone. Around his wife, at the office, he was like a thief; in the hands of the marvelous deity of whims who sails her boat over the banks of the earth, of household and society, Malloban's heart seemed to lie inert like a leech in the bowl of a water-pipe.

Utpala's conspicuous lack of concern suits him fine; he's killed a cat, the tiger's auntie, in his room; in the violence and heartlessness of a golden tigress, he finds a profound and perverted satisfaction. In the disorder and misery of the downstairs room, corroborating again and again his designation of himself as a depraved, abandoned husband, he is pleased; counting himself a misjudged man, unloved, deceived, his heart is lightened; if life's ill winds, misfortune, misjudgment, unlove run dry, then there's nowhere to go.

"You're not eating fish these days?"

"They stink," said Malloban.

"What do you mean, Thakur cooks them up nicely with onions and spices."

"He doesn't fry them well—" said Malloban for the sake of saying something.

"You want to eat them burnt?"

"No, no—" said Malloban, spreading his fingers and making a fist, spreading his fingers and making a fist. "It's frozen fish, after all, it's like wood. I can't stomach it."

"This is definitely not frozen fish. It's excellent. Fresh. From a tank. You buy it yourself, and you can't tell?"

Malloban didn't say anything.

"You can try koi fish. It's really nice."

But Malloban began to do without fish. Some days he eats yogurt; some days he doesn't; he eats negligently. He's not attached to his wife anymore. He doesn't say much. No complaints, no objections, no oil, no part in his hair. Anyone else would have grabbed him and pestered him: "Open up and tell me," "What is all this," "What's eating at you," "If you don't eat up, I won't let you go." But Utpala didn't seem to notice anything; fine; nobody pressed Malloban's hand and ruined the peaceful purity of his heart and blood. The dead certainty he wanted, he got; so he wants to pull out his venomous fangs? He wants to stay in the snake-charmer's basket? Let him. No one tried to stop him. No hitch.

But the murder of a kitten—even in the life of a man like Malloban, the acuteness of the unpalatable criminality of this act—wore away, abraded by days and nights. He got his old life back. Now and then, of course, he thought of the kitten, but his own life had a much stronger appeal. Fish, meat, eggs, office, newspaper, money troubles, his wife's this-that-and-the-other, open air, Goldighi, cheroot—he lost himself among all sorts of streams. He became a regular, mundane man again. Some days, lying awake far too late at night, Malloban felt: his life grunts and wallows in the mud and slime all day like a pig; the death of the kitten has given him a splendid release: he has risen far above his wife's aversion to affection, his mind has acquired a facile self-dependence such that at any moment he could send in his resignation at the office and go away, the lightness of a bird had come into his body of flesh and blood, as if he could rise up and fly away, as if none of life's contempt, desire, greed, nothing of it could touch him anymore; like silk-cotton broken off from the stem, floating in the ineffableness of village afternoons and evenings as spring turns to summer in the months of Chot-Boshekh, he had tasted a strange slow release in the blue of blueness, in sun and sunlight, in the feathers of birds on the roads of the sky, in the wings of bees, in some still blue otherworld. But in the daytime, these things don't stick with him; even if they do come to mind, they don't leave the same kind of mark.

And this is as it should be. For a man like Malloban, it's natural to spend the days of his life like any other man, in the house or office. Even his nights might have gone by like theirs, if an "excellent" woman like Utpala hadn't gotten in the way. Once involved with her, his life had gone on constantly buffeted by shocks, blows, and realizations. If not for that, he would have filled his house with offspring like the Maiti, De, Gorgori, and Guin Babus at his office, made house with a sindur-smudged loose-toothed bangled specter of a wife. But with Utpala, his life is not like that. It's not like theirs—it's something else.

On Sunday morning Malloban said to the maid, "Call your mistress for a minute." He had to send the maid upstairs three or four times.

Utpala came downstairs; she said, "Aren't you ashamed of yourself?"

"Why?"

"You sent the maid to call me?"

"There were people with you, I couldn't go and call you myself."

"Couldn't you wait until people left? What I do and don't do upstairs—you'll sit downstairs and play the rebel, turning over all those Ganeshas! Fine, pot-bellied Ganesh—"

"Never mind, they've left—"

"You drove them away—"

"The reason I called you—I've been thinking for several days that I have to talk to you about this room of mine. You see the state it's in, all upside down."

Utpala said, not looking at the room, "So what am I supposed to do about it!"

"I'm telling you to tidy it up a bit—"

Contemplating Malloban's blatant stupidity, Utpala didn't say anything more.

"The people who were upstairs, have they left?"

Without answering this question, Utpala was about to go upstairs; as soon as she lifted her foot to leave, some mysterious thing plopped down on the foot, it broke and spilled out, sparing the slipper, on the flesh, on the skin of Utpala's foot. Recoiling, she glanced at the windowsill and saw the bird; her eyes seemed to want to stick to the silly stupid bird, like Malloban's twin; what a strange place the egg fell in, maybe the bird unknowingly knocked it off, in its excessive strutting, pacing, flapping of wings; what happened, how the egg fell, broke, the bird has no idea, it has no consciousness of the lost, ruined egg; it's just going in circles on the windowsill, swelling its throat and going bok-brukom-brukom-brukom-brukir-rorom-rirom-rorom-bruk. When Utpala clapped her hands loudly, another bird came out from behind a beam; the two birds flew away together.

Looking at her own filthy foot, on the floor, in the midst of bird droppings and feathers and the dribble of the broken egg, Utpala said, "I see this flock of wild pigeons is renting this warehouse with tempered gold—"

"That they are," Malloban said before she had finished. He said in a very calm and meditative tone, "After all, what can you expect of birds. Humans are the real devils, not birds, otherwise would the world be like this? No, I don't say anything to those birds."

"I'll set out a trap. I'll catch every one of them and give them to Thakur. These plump doves' meat is good to eat—"

"I killed a kitten one day," said Malloban. It was unclear if he had heard what Utpala said. "From then on, I've begun to be very careful with these things. I don't say anything to all these creatures."

"Who killed a kitten?"

"I did." Malloban closed his eyes a little.

"When?"

"Oh, five days ago."

"Where?"

"Here in this room."

"But I didn't see it?"

"It was two in the morning, someone dropped it in here. The kitten's crying woke me up. Then—" He stopped.

"You pounded it to death—"

Malloban looked at Utpala's face once; he took a cheroot out of his pocket, closed his eyes, and looked inside himself; everything surfaced like a magic-lantern picture on a wet screen; that night, that kitten, the way he had (the picture started) grabbed the kitten with such ugly, honed, unnatural skill—how he had blindly flung it at the wall, how the kitten had died moaning—staring at all that for a few moments, his teeth clenched in utmost compassion, Malloban said, "When will I become human, that's what I'm thinking!? I've never been able to become one, even today, by any means. I'm trying—or am I? I don't say anything to the birds; they're making a mess of the whole room; it's no end of trouble, true, but so what? I keep to myself; I give them flattened rice, they like to eat barley, I scatter it on the floor, they eat and shit, shit and eat; leaving aside one or two, almost all humans do worse than them." Climbing the stairs of logic as he spoke, in the end Malloban could not help looking at Utpala's foot, the foot soiled by the runny dribble of the broken egg—

"But these birds . . ." After running his eyes all over and around Utpala for quite a while, Malloban said, " . . . they're completely thoughtless about laying eggs. They patter down like nuts from a patbadam tree. Every day they have losses—"

Malloban kept quiet for a few moments, lit the cheroot in his hand and began to count the many unruly waves in the earth and sky, arranging them according to some mysterious direction, saw pearls and coral blaze up and become crests of waves, and a good long while later he said, addressing that light, "But is it right to shoot them with a slingshot, just for that? It's not right."

Then he said, becoming lucid, "Is that blue sari of yours all right—it hasn't gotten wet, has it?"

"Aha, how well this peacock-throat blue suits you—" Malloban was thinking, "like Brihannala teaching Uttara to dance. In the spell of the dance, Brihannala and Uttara have become one—who is Utpala and who is Brihannala—" Utpala is looking indescribable—and yet she is standing, she is not actually dancing, or even moving; and yet Utpala looks as if she's standing on a razor's edge—the way a woman looks sublime if men deem her an ideal beauty.

"Can you make me a few pillowcases? If you can, I'll bring a few yards of markin cloth."

Utpala was ready with an answer: "Forget it, you can just drop it off at the tailor's house."

When his wife went upstairs, he went with her.

Once there he said, "Will you give me a paan? I thought I'd give it up. But I can't control the craving."

But Utpala didn't budge; sitting on a deck chair on the roof, in the sunlight and air, she tilted her neck and began to undo her braid! Seeing Utpala's body exude relaxation, a slow, reputable, intoxicating sense of pleasure was spreading down through Malloban's own joints and flesh. But it was no use staying upstairs any longer, Malloban felt; now he should go downstairs.

Going downstairs, Malloban decided he would clean up the room himself. Then he thought he would get the maid to do it. The maid was busy in the kitchen. Malloban lit a beedi and thought, what's the use of cleaning up!

But the next moment, he started cleaning up himself. In all that disorder and dirt, he started feeling peevish; but he didn't bother to move mountains, to get the room as impeccably clean as he had the other day; he swept the room, set things straight, changed the sheets, dropped off the dirty clothes in a laundry close by, and considered his work done.

The nights are extremely cold; all his socks are torn, he hasn't managed to buy a pullover, the woolen wrap he has on is in tatters, ravaged by oil, water, sun, and wind, he has even put on a few patches, it looks awful, makes him feel like buying a new wrap, there's no end of tears in the black-streaked mosquito net, dirty rotten bedbugs are swarming around, the mosquito net has become a huge jungle of sapped fibers.

After dinner, sitting in a cold tin chair in the downstairs room, Malloban was thinking: forget it, what's the use of leading this patchwork life, of use to whom?

Sitting on the bed, he thought: life is full of sudden tugs like that. Lying down, Malloban was thinking: who but me would go to bed now? Sitting and talking, telling stories—then in the winter night—the whole winter night: couldn't I have had a wife like that? I'm like a chicken in the cold current of a flash flood who wants to swim like a swan, wants to fly like a falcon. Such is my capsized life. But I've got far too much self-love: as if there were no other individual in the world, as if the history of people and time being made by a sea of individuals were nothing. Wrapping himself in the blanket, in the deepest of winter nights, the sound of today, of the ever-existing, of the sea of individuals—that which has been cleansed by lack of individuality, and gone, dragging him along like a fleck of foam, from darkness quite possibly into even more pervasive darkness—he could hear its tone; so that his mind became as if illuminated; slowly surrendering itself to the strange totality of time, his mind kept growing still . . .

So still that he fell asleep.

SEVENTEEN

At the end of the month of Poush, Mejda's family arrived.

Malloban went to stay in a "mess." Not exactly a mess—a middle-of-the-road boarding house. He had a separate room and tidied it up nicely. Mejda and Bouthan didn't want to let go of him for anything, but still, after thinking it through from every angle, he ended up going to the mess.

He didn't feel particularly inclined to acquaint himself with people at the mess. He came back from the office and thought about his own life's upheaval—until he could hear the distant sea-sound of surpassing the individual; as he waited to hear that sound, the night advanced—sleep overcame him beforehand; these days he hardly ever heard that sound, it didn't come, didn't want to be captured clearly. The Goldighi was close by—he went out. Some days he dropped by his own house to check on things—took a look around, enjoyed Mejda and Bouthan's candid sweet talk. They're such splendid people—maybe they're quarreling about little things, but at the same time it's as if there's one pulse tugging at both of them, like a pair of boshontobouri birds with human bodies and consciousness, outside the nest, then a moment later inside the nest—in every word, the essence of love, coated with the sugar-candy of sex, is expressed. Malloban finds it not bad to look at, that is, bad, somehow ugly: because, forgetting the water-mass of individuals, they give the individual, what has or hasn't happened to oneself, the most importance.

Sensing this, wanting to merge into the traceless mass of water and sunlight of the water-mass of individuals, as if he'd had a little bhang and was feeling good, with a taste in his mouth just like that, in a sweet voice, Malloban says, "Mejda, you two aren't having any trouble with the sleeping arrangements, are you?"

"No. Here we've got this nice big bed, rigged up with a mosquito net."

"You sleep there alone, I take it?"

"No."

"Your children sleep with you?"

"They sleep downstairs—with their aunt."

Mejda said, "She and I sleep here together. I can't sleep alone in bed—without at least the rustling of a sari beside me, it's no go. You understand . . ."

Malloban waved a gnat away from his temple.

Mejda said, clearing his throat, "There should be a nice warmth all around the bed, you know . . . Haha . . ."

Mejobouthan came into the room pounding paan with an iron pestle and mortar, rolled some little balls of pounded paan and set them down in front of Biraj Babu. Then she washed her hands and sat down right up against Biraj Babu's thigh—she's not shy. She wrapped the muffler snugly around Biraj's neck and said, "It's awfully cold;" taking out a pair of chocolate-colored socks from under the pillow, she put them onto Biraj Mittir's elephantiac left leg and his slender right leg with the expertise of middle-aged fingers—as if coming up from drippings sweeter than the drippings of a candle.

Back at the mess, Malloban felt it was an embarrassment that he had no one, nothing. The place is full of young men, and the kind of people who are always drooling after a certain kind of physical pleasure; they go out at night: where do they stay—what do they do? Some days they come back in the small hours of the night, sometimes they don't. Even the residents who don't spend their nights out still drool over a certain kind of physical-glandular pleasure, lying in bed right there at the mess. Year after year, they spend their whole lives in the mess. They have nowhere else to go—nothing else—no strength to make a home—

He lay down on the bed; but the next instant he sat up again. He started pacing on the veranda. He went to the reservoir. He came back from there. He took a newspaper; he set it down; he lit a cheroot; it went out; did the cook bring the rice yet?

The next morning, on the railing of Malloban's room at the mess, a few crows were cawing. Like his wife would shoo away flies, Malloban shooed them away by clapping his hands and shouting ha-ha. A gentleman from next door came out and said, "You see, sir, what a nuisance they are! Yesterday I bought eight annas' worth of kochuri-halua, put it on the table, and went to wash my face, and in that short time they came in and whisked away the carton of food—"

"These crows?"

"Yes sir."

"That's awfully impolite—"

But Malloban felt like calling these crows and giving them something to eat—since he'd driven them away, he felt a kind of emptiness. Every morning, long before he gets out of bed, the crows come and sit on this railing on the western side and caw. Lying in bed, he remembers his country town—his mother; that house thatched with straw—a winter dawn just like this—crows cawing just like this. Where has it all gone?

Malloban had gone back into his room and sat down by the table and was thinking this. Just then, through the fog, a lone crow flew over and sat down again by Malloban's room, on the railing of the terrace facing the tramline. Malloban sat in one place looking at the crow for a long time—he was listening to it caw. In the country, there are ravens and common crows; in Kolkata, only common crows—he hasn't seen any ravens. He hasn't seen a raven for a long time; he'd seen one in a huge advertisement on the main road; it wants to peck open the tight lid of a bottle of liquor—the fragrance of a famous French brand of alcohol has crazed the creature. The raven of the liquor advertisement, though, is worth looking up at: in one glance, it brought up the sky and air, birds and animals, society and perception of several years of his life.

The crow flew off through the fog—towards the reservoir—into a neem tree. It feels nice to fly off like that.

In the house in the country, they had a huge courtyard, covered with grass, here and there the hard white ground peeking out, all day long sunlight, shade, shadows of clouds, shadows of the wings of hawks in the sky playing over it— rebounding in sunlight, in speed, like restless iron sulphate.

Shalikh birds flew in over the courtyard; herons jumped down onto the straw roof—on the way from this pond to that pond, the scent of water in their wings, the glow of color on their beaks, their startled eyes gazing into the distance, into the blueness. So many tall, tall trees stood surrounding the courtyard; all winter long the forest of jarul, jhau, patbadam and mango, the jungle of neem and hijol, rang with the calls of doves—if he turned his back to the sun and leaned back a little, his whole body filled with sleep at that bird's call. Sometimes the doves came down into the courtyard, somehow like machines, like tiny dhenkis from the birds' country, the doves' tails went up and down, up and down—going ghur-ghurghur-ghur they whirred around on the field and the grass—what were they looking for— what did they want? It seems the world never remembers all those birds in the fog of that winter morning twenty-five or thirty years ago; today's world is just a strange unworld in the labyrinth of Kolkata's commercial power. Puffing out their throats of a color like weak coffee or cocoa, so many common crows came flying to the straw roof, the courtyard; they whizzed off across the cold water, just skimming the rivers and ponds, reflected blurrily in the water, whirring off from who knows where—where are they? From the direction of the morning fog, they went flying far off in the other direction to draw out the very earth, those crows, to bring out the shining sun for everyone—even those who aren't crows, aren't birds—ko-ko-koko—what a racket of a hundred consciousnesses, arbitration, solitude.

EIGHTEEN

On the day of Saraswati Pujo, in a room right by Malloban's, some boarding house residents got drunk together. In a hall-like room, they had a dancing girl perform. The maid sat side by side with the babus and watched the dance; Malloban was taken aback when he saw that the maid wasn't shy at all—as if she were quite used to this; sometimes she acts like the babus' mother, sometimes she's someone's own wife, so it seems, sometimes she's like everyone's intimate friend—gentle, affectionate, eager to take everyone tidily in hand, dripping with easy, cheap coquetry. And tomorrow morning, she'll settle down to scrubbing dishes again. Then Malloban for one won't even bother to look at this imbecilic face of hers. Will even these babus give her a second glance then? But tonight, she's the life of the party. It's not a bad party either. She chews a paan—puffs on a cigarette—flits from one man to another with her gossip routine—if not for her, for quite a few babus, the better part of tonight's fun would have been spoiled.

Thinking this and that, at the height of his thoughts, Malloban was thinking: what does all this have to do with Saraswati Pujo? Liquor, dancing girls, maids—who needs all this? But in this gathering, he was perhaps the only one thinking like that. And he alone is so alone! Silent—as if he's made a faux pas that stands out against all the others' clamor and glamour. But this much is certain, he has no contempt for any of them.

He didn't have any drinks, of course, and for some reason he didn't even have a smoke, he just chewed a couple of paan, but then again, he didn't get up and leave the gathering: he sat through all the dancing and singing. Now everyone was having a fine time with the maid Gayamati (what's that supposed to mean, that name?), but looking at this girl's face—like a carp-face, snapper-face, spider-legs, drongo-legs—Malloban felt a deep sorrow from time to time. The electric light shines from time to time into the girl's dim eyes, she suffers in the harsh stiff heat of the lamp, he feels such sorrow; the girl's sari-end slips off her head, a tiny bun like a little girl's pops out—he feels greatly pained; stuck on a broken chair, the girl's sari gets a long tear, she doesn't notice herself, but Malloban's sympathy pains are terrible—terrible; the girl, puffing on a cigarette, keeps putting a hand to her chest and coughing—Malloban feels discomfited; when the girl coughs, her two eyes grow round like a fish's—it looks ugly—it bothers Malloban, how he suffers for this strange skeletal girl, for this person alone. Malloban wasn't feeling so good, he was speechless, thinking, she's smoking so much, what pleasure is Gayamati getting out of this, she's smoking and coughing, she's coughing so much and still she's dragging so hard on the cigarette, it would have seemed so strange and amusing, but it had started to distress him.

Four or five babus together took the maid into a separate room. About to go back to his own room, Malloban turned and saw them plying the maid with alcohol.

Walking, Malloban thought: what kind of fun is this? Still, he didn't make any effort to protest; he doesn't have the cheek to protest, doesn't have the strength or the glory; or the urge; he knows, this kind of misbehavior has gone on in many parts of the world; nobody can obstruct it, it doesn't bother about anybody's obstruction.

Climbing up to the third floor, he paced on the veranda in the dark for a while. Then he came close to the railing and looked down once; he saw that same maid sitting under the tap with her head down, vomiting; beside her only two companions. The mess cook Bamdeb—a long gaunt man—with a face a lot like Trailokya's—is sitting at a little distance, one leg crossed over the other and his back against the wall, taking pinches of snuff with a detached look— now and then, he lifts his eyes as if covered in cobwebs and looks at the maid. Sitting by the maid and stroking her back is Purno Kurmi from Chapra District. The man is short, dark, pockmarked, with very long, exceedingly white teeth that nevertheless give off an unpleasant smell; but he's a cheerful person; more than anyone in this mess, he loves this maid. Whom does the maid love? Not Purno, not the cook; whom, Malloban doesn't know. Purno's put his mind to the business of love today; he's got some money in his pocket today; he'll do business with the maid tonight.

From above, a symphony of several voices suddenly rang out all at once: "Purno! Purno! Purno!"

Maybe they've run out of liquor upstairs or meat or soda water; Purno will have to run to the store right away.

Gayamati said, "Go on, Purno, Bamdeb's sitting right here—that's enough—you come around one-thirty."

Purno stretched, sitting down, bending his body and wriggling like an earthworm in newly overturned earth. Then he suddenly left.

Bamdeb said, "You've doomed yourself, you've become a whore. But I'm a Chokkotti Bamun, remember, I can't give you money like Purno."

"You may be a Bamun, I'm no Haari's daughter either, my dad's name is Sidhu Sarkar—"

"That same Sidhu from Gobora? The one that used to come around and you'd feed him?"

"Sidhu Sarkar from Kasba. You've never seen him."

"A Sarkar is a kind of Kayet, sure," Bamdeb let out a belch and said, "Forget it. Listen, Kayet girl, you threw up!"

"I'm not used to all that stuff."

"You got a bit out of hand, Gaya. Are you going to throw up any more?"

"No."

"If you feel like throwing up, tell me. As soon as I put my hand on your back, it'll all come tumbling out—"

"No! It's settled down," Gayamati said. "My insides are chilled to the bone."

"Then come on—"

"Where?"

"Where else, the babus are done eating. You scarfed it all up and barfed it all out, I got my fill just looking. Don't need to eat anything else!"

"Here, here, eat up," Gaya said with a great display of caring. "You just go on pinching snuff. Come on, get up."

"I don't feel like it," Bamdeb said, somehow crumpling his face. "Cooking all day long over the hot stove, watching you vomit—the pot of food dried up into wood in my belly, Gaya!"

Gaya, who had been sitting under the tap all this time, gave her head a slight shake and said, standing up, "I tell you, bapu, I don't feel good. You're sort of a snob, bapu, you've gotten so snobbish. I'm calling you by your name, Bamdeb—won't you eat? Really, you won't eat anything!"

"No! I won't eat 'anna' anymore today, I'll eat 'mishtanna'—no rice, only sweets!"

"Fine! Fine!!" Gaya doubled over with laughter, like a sickly shaora tree in a gust of wind. She came and sat down right by Bamdeb on the terrace.

"Did Purno say he'd come back at one-thirty?"

"Who knows what he said." Sensing danger, seeking Bamdeb's counsel, clearing up her two weary unclear eyes a bit in Bamdeb's familiar gaze, Gaya said, "He's trouble, Purno. I won't let him to get too familiar tonight."

"Well, what else! You've got a woman's body, Gaya. He'd love to make five of it."

Like Shibiraja offering his own flesh to the hawk to protect the dove, Bamdeb said, "Behula won't have to stay up all night on account of those black cobras, Gaya. I'll take you to a place he won't even get his fangs into."

Malloban heard this on his way into his own room.

The boarding house food is not agreeing with Malloban. They make some kind of ghyanto with a few stalks, skins, snippets, and slices, they don't know how to cook, they're stingy with oil and spices, they never bring good fish and vegetables from the bazaar; "If they keep this up, I'm going to leave this mess."

One day the manager brought a few goats, three or so, and tied them up in a shed next to a room downstairs. All day long, the goats bleat; Malloban thinks, worrying in an unclear, uncommon-to-humans sort of way: how the poor things must suffer in this nitrous cold! Maybe they've sensed that they're going to die soon; as if they're sensing a meaty smell, of their own death; that this is the work of human hands, they've understood. Creation, Malloban went on thinking—nature gave them such a fatal sexual appetite only to make offspring, only to destroy them. Taking advantage of their excessive lust, humans use these creatures only to increase their race, cut them down—and eat them. What in all of creation is more of a devil than a human! Devils. Devils.

Malloban's mind went somehow crooked, twisted, he felt like going to the manager and saying, "Let them go, Mr. Achajji. I'll give you your money." But what if he did let them go, someone else would catch and eat them. Could they escape human society unscathed with that nice meat of theirs? Where would they go? Into what billygoat-universe? There's no such thing.

The manager Manohar Achajji has brought three nice, well-fed, oil-slick goats. Everyone in the boarding house is so eager to eat the goat meat, such intense demands keep coming from all sides about when the goats will be butchered, everyone's mouths are watering so much, Malloban realized as he thought about it that he is one human among them, humans eat meat with a clear conscience, just as they eat fruit and grain with a clear

conscience; only one or two among them feel pangs of
conscience; as humans maybe that's unnatural; to himself
he seemed a bit unnatural—as a human. Malloban has
decided, he won't eat these goats' meat.

But four or five days later, the manager sold off the
three goats; the cook brought rice and bitter potol-vine
curry, a stew of small catfish, and black gram dal. Malloban
felt somehow dispirited, he said, "Thakur, we weren't fated
to have meat." But as he ate, Malloban scolded himself: for
shame, is my eating meat more important than the lives of
three creatures?

The next day, two goats appeared in the shed again;
Malloban got a bit of a shock; he thought: what is this?
Eating his rice, he thought: that meat is not for us to eat,
maybe the manager's taken up the goat trade. As he thinks—
all his preparations for ascetic experience have somehow
gone dead.

In the evening, the manager said to Nikunjo Pakorashi,
"No, no, I'll butcher this goat tomorrow."

Hearing this, Malloban felt somehow encouraged.
Going around the Goldighi, he thought: life has become
so filthy today—just a few pieces of meat, and for that, the
death of two creatures has become a thing of such hope
and confidence for me! But this is natural—like jackals and
cats, cheetahs and fat tigers, humans are violent too. Being
human, by nature, he doesn't have the choice to go around
being nonviolent. But still Malloban resolved not to eat
this meat.

And he didn't eat it, but it took him quite an effort
to send back the bowl of meat; the three spoonfuls of
watery rabdi had no taste at all, a very active grudge made

him think aggressive thoughts about the manager and the cook. Human life is not at all simple or beautiful, Malloban's own life is not straightforward, not honest, he was realizing.

NINETEEN

Lying in bed at the mess throughout the winter night, sometimes he sleeps very well. Sometimes he doesn't sleep so well—he paces on the veranda. He feels like going home the very next day; in the morning, he still feels the same way. But the later into the day it gets, the more he can understand the unnaturalness of that desire; he adapts himself to the monotonous life of the mess. Some days at the end of the night, in deep darkness and cold, in bed ready for sleep, it feels so good; the hubbub, commotion, and tumult of life seem so meaningless that he's afraid to remember the light of morning.

Sometimes he dreams very beautiful dreams.

He's spent many a night in the boarding house splendidly. One thing he loves: a tall slender youth, in the small hours of every night, walks down the street reciting all kinds of English and Bengali poems; agitated, Malloban thinks—this boy's life has its grandeur, for sure, but it's not a shallow thing, it's genuinely deep; if only he had a life like his.

In the morning, through the fog, a few crows come flying over to the railing of Malloban's veranda, through the random breaks in the fog, they spread their wings and disappear in the direction of the deodar and neem trees that ring the reservoir; as if nature's compass-heart is stirring. Malloban feels a touch of magic. And yet it's not supernatural—how naturally ancient, this light, the birds, the sky's language.

One morning a crow came and sat on Malloban's railing. The crow turned around and looked at Malloban, tried to call out many times, but the bird's voice wouldn't come out of its throat for anything. He's caught a cold and it's settled in his throat. Maybe the bird doesn't understand that he'll get his voice back again. He's lost his voice, who knows what he's thinking. Malloban tossed him a bit of biscuit. The crow came into the room and ate the bits and pieces of biscuit, hopping about with a crunching sound amid the papers. The crow hung around in Malloban's room for a long time—ate a few biscuit pieces.

A week or so later, pacing on the boarding-house veranda, Malloban saw a gentleman sitting quietly beside a pile of luggage in a big, dark, dank room in the boarding house. The room and the man are a match—looking at the two of them, life's hope and faith fall to the ground, spent. Over the next few days, Malloban saw that the gentleman just sat quietly, not talking to anybody, nothing. Sometimes he put on his glasses and picked up a book or two, but he didn't seem to get very far in his reading.

One day, Malloban entered the gentleman's room and said, "How are you?"

Slipping his glasses off the tip of his nose like the leg of some disheveled tailorbird and rubbing both eyes with the fingers of his left hand, the gentleman said, "I'm not well."

"What's wrong?"

"I've had a fever these past few days—"

"Then why are you staying in this room—"

"Where else would I stay?"

Taking a tangled bundle of rags out of his pocket and cleaning the mucus from his eye, the gentleman said, "Since the day my wife died, I haven't been home—"

"Oh!"

"It's only been five months or so since she died. Twenty-five or thirty years at a stretch, we made our home together. No children. Now I don't feel comfortable in that unlucky house. That's why I came here, to see auspicious faces—you people's!"

He asked Malloban, "Your wife is alive, isn't she?"

"She is—she is—" Malloban said in a trembling voice, as if reciting a mantra.

"She's gone to her father's house, I take it?"

Malloban hesitated for a moment, looking at the veranda railing, where the crows came and sat, and at the direction they flew off in through the narrow path of fog to the neem trees at the reservoir.

"Really, you won't understand my position," the gentleman said, putting a hand on his salt-and-pepper beard. "No one understands. My wife went off with a hamper of white wool in her hand, laughing—"

"A basket of wool?"

"Yes, she was knitting a vest for me—"

"Oh!"

"She was knitting in the month of Ashshin—before the cold set in, out in the country. Last winter, I whined a lot about not having a warm shirt. No, I didn't whine that much, I'm not that much of a child, but I shivered a lot. I'd really gotten awfully shy of the cold, she sensed it. So this time she was making me a wool shirt—"

The gentleman kept quiet for a few moments, then said, "She told me, I'll make you a vest in two days flat, and she started working those crochet needles night and day. Four hands all told, you understand, sir—knit a vest with two hands, do the household chores with the other two. Grinding spices and chopping vegetables for cooking, drawing hot water for my bath, giving me an oil massage for my rheumatic back—hornbill oil—my name is Bipin Ghosh—"

Bipin Babu said, "That's another history, I'll tell you later how she got ahold of hornbill oil. It's not a thing you can get from a hawker on his rounds, it's the genuine article, my wife had a hand in that too—"

"That's what they call a wife," Malloban said, jerking his eyes as if turning a joist, staring at Bipin Ghosh the whole time, with a strong feeling of gratification. "Not just any Panchi or Khendi, not just anyone's wife—they're all unripe Totapuri mangoes, in the end. You got the Kishanbhog in flesh and bone, dada, aha-ha, and she left you!"

"She came to me with the blessings of people like you." Even though he'd been touched in a sore spot, Bipin Babu steadied himself and said, "And she's gone with your blessing on her head—"

Malloban, staring speechlessly, saw that Bipin Babu didn't show the slightest sign of weakness, as if the man had had his nerves, glands, and breastbone made in a factory.

"In two days, she'd almost finished the wool shirt—a vest this big, you can see I've got a hefty frame—"

Bipin Ghosh took a box of substandard cigarettes out of his pocket, held it out to Malloban and said, "Here, sir—"

Lighting one himself, he said, "When the vest was almost done, I got her into a special domestic conversation—I mean, I'd reserved her for that night in advance. She somehow made mistakes here and there in the knitting—had to unravel the whole shirt again—"

"Aha!"

"She desperately started knitting again. On top of that, it was a bit of a strain for her that night, to fulfill my demands. Things got a little out of hand—almost until the end of the night. Her blood pressure went up quite a bit. In the morning, she got up a little late and stood in the sun with that same wool and those crochet needles. I was sitting on a stool facing her. She was talking and laughing with me, and that was it. She suddenly fell down in a faint. Then it happened—"

Bipin Ghosh didn't say anything more. He finished a cigarette, two cigarettes, three cigarettes. Then Bipin Ghosh looked at Malloban and put a hand on his own collarbone. His two eyes started dancing as if they would never stop. Then he put on a Nehru jacket and quickly went downstairs.

TWENTY

Of course, as soon as Malloban left the office that day, he went straight to Utpala. He went and said, "No, I can't stay at the mess any longer."

"Why?"

"I'm coming home today."

"Where are you going to stay, tell me?"

"Where I was—on the ground floor—"

"There's no room there."

Malloban said, "I'll just lurk in some corner of the house, you won't have to worry about that—"

"Have you lost it?" Utpala said in a bit of a temper. "There's no place to hide in this house. You're in fine form, though. There won't be room enough. You'll have to stay in the mess. After all, I can't drive them away."

"But this is my house."

"If that's what you think, then Mejda and I will rent another flat—"

"No, no, I'm not saying that—" Realizing that he'd said a bit too much, Malloban said, "If you go away, what am I going to do in this house. That would be no different from a mess!"

For the sake of saying something, Malloban said, "Lying in bed at the mess some nights, I lose confidence. I think, if I die, then I'll never see you—"

Looking at Utpala's face, Malloban felt he was at a disadvantage; not bothering to finish with the subject he'd brought up, he said, "By the way, you've paid the premiums on my life insurance policy, haven't you? I left the money with you—"

"It's been spent."

"Spent! That's not surprising! These days this house is burning on Ravana's pyre, isn't it?"

"Mejda said you should take another policy."

"That's not going to happen."

"Why, you're the right age."

"No, not for the age."

"Mejda said you won't get hung up on the medical test. He can make sure you pass."

"He's an agent, he's got his interests," Malloban said, letting out a little (it seemed to Utpala) facetious, irreverent laugh like a precocious child. He sat there with a sly look on his face—it seems it's not as easy as Utpala thought to hit Malloban where it hurts.

"You should get one from Mejda's company."

"I know that. If I could, I would. If the two we have don't lapse, that's enough for us—"

"No, no, go on and get one."

"There's no money!"

"I'll be the judge of that."

"Fine then, see to it. But as I was saying, staying in the mess just dries me up—some nights. I did stay in a mess before we got married, but now I'm not up to it, not for anything. The mess babus say, you're having a fine time grazing in forests and jungles, dada, like an elephant, and now you want to be penned!"

"That's what they say, do they?"

"I'm a house elephant," Malloban said, "What am I going to do with a forest?"

"That's what you say, do you? You call yourself a palace elephant?"

"I call myself a temple elephant—"

"Why a temple elephant?"

"Oh, I say whatever comes into my mouth. I'll move out of the mess tomorrow."

"Since you moved to the mess, your health has improved," Utpala said, "Don't do anything hasty. Stay there for a few days. You've been in messes all your life, you've gotten acclimatized to messes; household life isn't suiting you too well. The other day I was straightening up that downstairs room for my nieces and nephews, and Mejobouthan said, I see that shalgram has left this place looking like a room in a mess—"

"Really? What did you say?"

"What could I say. The most intelligent thing to say is nothing."

Malloban sent a sweeping glance all around, let out a burp, gave the corner of his mustache a twist and said, "Mejobouthan can say whatever she likes. I have a right to live with my wife and children however I please. Why should I throw away my own property and go to a mess?"

Malloban lit a cheroot and said, "Is Mejobouthan going to send her husband off to a mess and enjoy herself?"

Utpala said, undoing her loose bun, lifting a bunch of hair in her hand and winding it into a tight bun, "It's hardly the same for them as it is for us—"

"Enough, enough." Not finding the demoness Shingshapa at hand, Malloban crushed the cheroot between his teeth and said, "I know this, that, and all the rest. I don't go invading other people's houses like your sister-in-law's husband. I'm going to live in my own way in my own house—I'll be a shalgram, I'll be a shivalinga—I'll be whatever I want—what's it to them—"

Utpala kept her temper and said coolly, "Fair enough. But not tomorrow. Come back in eight or ten days, we're clearing out the downstairs room for you—"

At that, Malloban's overheated heart became pleasantly warm. "Eight or ten days?"

"Yes."

"The downstairs room is being cleared out?"

"That's right."

"Who's doing it?"

"We are."

Arrangements are being made for him, Utpala herself is making arrangements, he's chewed the cheroot to pieces for nothing. Throwing away the wasted cheroot, he took a fresh one out of his pocket and said, "I don't believe in all that, but as a fact it's not a bad thing—"

"What thing?"

"Oh, that—we were married according to the auspicious union of the planets—even if your Mejda curled his lip, your other brothers were happy—your father too, extremely—"

Malloban built up a nice blazing fire in his cheroot, shrewdly taking drags in the gaps in the conversation. Utpala said in a hard voice, with a slightly muffled laugh, "Who? It was Poresh Ghotok who settled it."

"Yes, he beat his brains over it for three nights."

"Auspicious union," Utpala said with a little gasp of laughter, in a lively voice like a shankhini, "Auspicious union—go tell Poresh Ghotok that the fruits and twigs and legs of marriages are over his head."

"You want to blow off the pundit!"

"I don't need punditry, I say what I feel."

"What is it you—feel?"

"I don't want to take this any farther," Utpala said, smoldering slightly, as if someone were fanning the flames. "Now you'll have to stay in the mess. I told you in eight or ten days the downstairs room might be cleared out; but that seems unlikely, it's bound to take at least a month and a half."

Utpala made a face as if to bare a row of pretty teeth and laugh, but she didn't laugh, she spoke seriously. In the blink of an eye, her row of teeth disappeared. Her two lips met and hardened like a tightly lidded box of sindur.

"How long will I have to stay in the mess?"

"As long as it takes."

"When are they leaving, Mejda and them?"

"How am I supposed to ask them that?"

"They should have thought about it themselves."

Utpala said, as if standing a few steps above Malloban, "Are you going to teach them that?"

Malloban's eye fell on the cheroot in his hand. Clamping the cheroot between his teeth, he started puffing. With so much puffing, a lot of ash has piled up in the mouth of the cheroot—even then, what can he do? He starts puffing again. A few moments passed, and then he remembered. He started telling Utpala the story of Bipin Ghosh! After the preamble, Utpala said, "Don't you smell milk burning?"

"No, I don't think so."

"There, I can smell it."

"No, no, listen to the story, oh, maybe the milk's boiled over next door—"

That it's next door, Utpala has figured out; she has a nose, she has ears, she has a number of other subtle bird-instincts and animal-experiences, that the cook next door has slipped out of the kitchen and is chitchatting with the paanseller, she has figured out, with her pricked-up eyes and ears, but still there's a grain of doubt left in Utpala's mind, she said, "If our milk burns, it'll be a disaster—Mejda's—"

"There's no milk on your stove. I know. I just came by way of the kitchen, Rangi's cooking a chyanchra—" Malloban said, taking the cheroot out of his mouth.

Utpala said, pressing a hand down on top of her great big bound-up bun (there's no tassel woven into her braid) of thick black hair, "Nothing doing, bapu, I don't have time to hear your Bipin Ghosh gossip. You believe all that because you're gullible. He's cheated you royally, Bipin Ghosh; I'm sure he's filched some of your cash."

Mortified, Malloban kept quiet for a few moments, then he said, "If he'd asked me for some money, I'd have given it, sure. But is Bipin Ghosh the type to ask for money? He's not. If you talked with him, you'd understand. The man's really lost everything. He sat there for ten minutes and smoked three cigarettes one after the other—didn't even say a word to me—then he touched his throat and his eyes and face went all—like a fighting cock that can't find his hen on the trash heap, he totally broke down, Bipin Ghosh. He put on his Nehru jacket and left without a word."

Malloban has become of one breath with Bipin Ghosh; as if it's his wife that's died, his home that's been broken, and still he has to gather the inner strength to bear it, as if to add a hoarse cough, with a brave face charged with emotion, Utpala's husband looked at her.

"Do apes like that Bipin Ghosh of yours really exist?"

"You called him an ape, Utpala?"

"He didn't filch anything from your pocket, did he?"

"Why would he do that? What are you thinking—"

"He didn't sell you a line and filch something, then, from a thickheaded man like you?" Utpala said with a sugary look, wrapping her arm once around Malloban's waist, "You've done well, then. I'll be needing some. How much have you got on you?" Wrapping her arm once around Malloban's neck with a sweet face and giving him a sudden tug, she said, "Whatever you've got, hand it over."

Malloban said, procrastinating, "I will. But today I don't feel like going back to the mess. We can manage something for one night."

Taking the money, Utpala said, "You can eat here tonight, at least."

"No, no, I'm not talking about eating, can I sleep here for a bit? Where do you sleep?"

"I need fifty rupees."

"All right, I'll get a loan—"

"When?"

"Tomorrow. Today I'm giving you twenty-five. Where does Monu sleep? And you?"

The next day Malloban came and said, "I didn't think I would come back here so soon."

Utpala wasn't saying anything.

"But you know, I couldn't help but come." Malloban pulled out a chair and sat down.

"You sat down there?"

"Why, what happened?"

"Don't you see I'm in the middle of something."

Malloban waved that off and said, "So go ahead—go ahead—I didn't come to stop you from working. Who's the blouse for?"

Utpala had taken the handle of the sewing machine lightly in her fist and was wondering whether to turn it. Setting the blouse straight under the needle, Utpala started running the machine.

"The sewing machine is your Lakshmi. See how it's whirling in your hand like Vishnu's discus, cutting right through Sati's body: wonderful!" Malloban said; he thought himself quite eloquent to have said that about cutting through Sati's body; the other Utpala he's carrying around on his shoulder in the science and agnosis of his own mind, she's cutting this Utpala up into little pieces.

Utpala has no trouble keeping herself occupied with the sewing machine, with the sitar or the esraj. "It's really boring at night in the mess. It would be nice if I learned to play the esraj."

"You want to play the esraj?"

"Why, can't I do it?"

"The man says, Hari Uncle, tuck in your loincloth; Hari Uncle says, where has my loincloth slipped, that I should tuck it in—" Utpala kept on running the machine. When the thread snapped suddenly, she paused a moment and fiddled with it, then said, "No, it hasn't snapped, it's fine."

"Is there thread on the bobbin?"

"There is, it's fine, it's as strong as the Howrah Bridge, here, move—don't bother me."

Malloban had been staring at Utpala's hand turning the wheel, true, but his mind was flying like reaped cotton in the month of Chot on so many hundreds of breezes—of bluenesses!

"The boys go speeding by on their bicycles—Benetola, Nabin Pal Lane, Potoldanga, College Street, Kolabagan, Hatibagan, Gayabagan—the crossroads of Chaurangi. Great fun, but some things I never could learn—to ride a bike, to speak Urdu, to stroll around from place to place in pajamas, sandals, and a sherwani coat, or in a western suit—"

Utpala, quietly running the machine, grew even more silent and detached.

"This office job's given me a beating. I feel like ditching everything and living my own way, you'll play the sitar, I'll listen—all day long."

Utpala took the blouse out from under the teeth of the machine and spread it out to look at it once; there's still a lot of sewing left to be done. Even if she had turned a deaf ear to the poetic flow of Malloban's narrative, she was listening with her inner ear by way of the subconscious.

"Suppose we have twenty or twenty-five years before us. Won't there be some variety in life within that time? What do you think, won't there be some variety? It will be good—life will go by all well and good? What do you think, dear?"

"You hope to live another twenty years?"

"I might live that long."

"What's the use of living that long?" Utpala gave most of her attention to the blouse, but still giving some attention to her own words, she said calmly, "I'm speaking for myself as well—what's possible and impossible for us in life, I understood long ago. Now I'll be satisfied if I can slip away in peace—"

Malloban felt somewhat chagrined and perturbed by what Utpala was saying. He unconsciously took a beedi out of his pocket and was about to light it, almost, but these days he didn't smoke beedis in front of his wife; he didn't even take out a cigarette, he said, "If someone has to say goodbye, it'll be me. You've got plenty to gain by staying alive. I lie in bed at night in the mess some days and think, think about you. You really haven't had much luck in life, have you? There are so many people, so much noise in your room day and night. Even if you sat in hell, there'd be a hundred "ruined moons" around you. Your Mejda and Bouthan—however happy they are to be with you, you're much happier to have them with you. What do you say?"

Malloban was talking with his eyes closed. Opening them, he looked at Utpala. She was working, she didn't have time to talk or to lift her face and look at him.

"Really, you had a lot of talents, and you used them well—" As he spoke, Malloban felt he could see his own mouth speaking; he's come face to face with his own face, the face just keeps moving its mouth, not reflected in Utpala's heart but deflected, how monstrously he's kept on moving his mouth, like a monkey at the zoo chewing roasted chickpeas nonstop. This is what his talking comes to? His expressing emotion?

Utpala was single-mindedly running the machine. It isn't that her memory isn't stirred, but the memory of some other sexual situation, with some other person? Like a drowsy stork, burying his face in the feathers of his own breast, Malloban was searching for some solution, but he couldn't come up with anything.

As if freeing his face from within the feathers and meat of his breast, Malloban said, "Forget it, let's neither of us talk about death anymore. Let's keep on living, however long time keeps us alive. Let's see what happens. It's good to have confidence. Why don't you teach me to play something—this esraj—"

"Himangshu Babu plays the esraj very well. Take him for a teacher."

"Him? Did I say I wanted to play the esraj on Himangshu Babu's neck?"

"Why, it's not hard. He comes all the time."

Malloban looked quietly for a few moments at Utpala's hands, the smell of petroleum, the cover of the sewing machine, the readied blouse, and said finally, "No! Not everyone is cut out for music, I was just talking."

He didn't bring up the esraj again. "I see Monu's turning into a toothpick! What's happening?"

"She's turning into a toothpick," Utpala said.

"What does she eat?"

"What do I know."

"Maybe nothing she eats is suiting her. She's got a stomach problem, that's why she's wasting away. Or is it that she can't even eat, she doesn't get anything good to eat?"

Utpala had opened a sewing book and was absorbed in some designs; whether she had heard or not what

Malloban has said or hasn't said, it was hard to tell; she didn't answer.

"Monu's health is going downhill."

"Is it?"

"She's half the size. Can't you tell?"

"Maybe she's sick," Utpala said. "Maybe she's got her father's mental sickness—"

Malloban looked at the sewing book and saw it was in English; it's not a book—maybe a journal; Utpala's flipping through the pages of the journal. She's bent over with her nose in the magazine. Utpala will get an MA in sewing, maybe she'll get a doctorate, but Monu, she's turning into the sutoshankh snake of the fairy tale—so skinny—such terrible dregs—like a stillborn. If things go on like this, while Malloban's still living at the mess—in this condition, in this house, it'll be hard to keep Monu going. It'll be hard.

"Monu has a bad liver—do you give her those liver pills?"

"No."

"Why?"

"That medicine got lost somewhere."

"Lost! Then I'll have to go buy some today."

"Sure."

Malloban said, managing to give his conversational style a touch of roguish heat, "What's the use of buying it—if it's not going to be fed to her."

"That's true too."

Not this way, not that way—sensing he needed to find the right way, Malloban said, "You're saying there's no room in this house."

"That's what I think."

"What if I put out a camp cot on the roof?"

"You can figure that out for yourself."

"What do you think?"

"We're looking for a house."

"Why?"

"I'm going to go stay in my father's house for a while. My oldest brother is coming to Kolkata—so is the youngest."

No one's looking for a house, no one's coming, Malloban knows that. Throwing the strange load of willful sin onto his back, he stood up. Utpala was busily running the machine.

Malloban went out.

TWENTY-ONE

Malloban went to the reservoir. He circled the reservoir for a long time. Then he went back to the mess. After eating, when he went to lie down, Malloban remembered he hadn't bought Monu's pills.

It was pretty late. There were still a couple of pharmacies open. He bought a bottle of liver pills and went straight up to the upstairs room to give them to Utpala. There he saw that Mejda, Mejobouthan and Utpala had finished eating and were all three of them sitting with their legs stretched out on the bed, talking and laughing, chewing paan and tobacco. Malloban gave the bottle of medicine to Utpala and was about to go downstairs. Mejda said, "Oh jamai, where are you running off to—oh jamai!"

Malloban went straight down to the downstairs room. He saw the children were all sleeping. He came and stood by Monu's bed; the little girl's body is lying there like a stick of jute—as if one puff could send it flying—that this body would put on flesh by any process—by any kind of process—does not seem possible; the kind of frame that can be hoped to regain its health from medicine, from going to some nice place for a change of air, this girl's body doesn't

have even that kind of frame. Just a few bones, not even like
bones—like dry matchsticks.

The mosquitoes are biting; Malloban spread out the
mosquito net with a whiff of air. He drew the blanket up
over Monu's chest.

Malloban's heart, on the verge of drying up, suddenly
filled—with what? Not desire—not a man's love for a
woman; nor for Monu—for this sole offspring of his, not only
common fatherly love, some kind of universal compassion
has come over him—for Monu, for all the children sleeping
here, for Bipin Ghosh's wife, for Bipin Ghosh, for Mejda,
for Bouthan, even for his own wife. At this moment he
felt no bitterness, no dullness. Sexual attraction or, beyond
sex, deep love—love for a woman—passing through all
these strata and snares, into the radiance of a solitary soul-
piercing all-encompassing mercy, Malloban became, for a
few moments, almost superhuman.

Going down to the street, Malloban felt, like great men,
that not love or desire, but compassion alone inlays humans
like drops of dew in the fire-artistry of all creation.

Love is a great thing indeed; love of a woman is greater
than love of a dancing-girl, greater than love of a woman is
love of everyone, a close attraction to the primordial soul.
But compassion? A worm, that dead kitten, Monu, Bipin
Ghosh's wife, Bipin Babu himself, even Malloban's own
wife—all of them, immersed in the compassion of Malloban's
heart, will become beloved of the primordial soul.

Walking towards the mess, Malloban suddenly stopped
short and said, "For shame, that's why I'm feeling so proud?
I'm feeling self-important just because a great compassion for
creation has entered my soul? No, no—there's no relation

between compassion and pride. This isn't love, it's the lowest of things, the least of things. I'm the vilest of all—the vilest—I'm worthy of everyone's pity, that everyone is the vessel of the highest soul's compassion, that is everyone is beloved of that soul—this feeling alone, this is compassion."

But lying in bed at the mess, slipping down into the warm threadbare quilt and the cold night, when compassion began to beat down on his love of women, love of worldly women, even his joints and flesh, then all the chickpea fields of his country childhood, the big pond, the room with a bamboo fence, the mattress of warm straw on winter nights, the fields soaked with dew like scattered spices, the rustling of owls' wings, and in the distance the best imaginable calls of black birds—breaking into the coffers of time, Malloban began to take each of them out. Ten or fifteen minutes later, Malloban felt, so many faces crowded around, so much trouble, such a terrible inextricableness— what a commotion!

Another few minutes later: even though the claims of a few other faces are no weaker, still, like a completely unexpected event for today's thoroughly temporal needs, a single face remains in his breast; that face is not his wife's.

At three in the morning, coming back from the water tank, shivering, Malloban was thinking: in the essential moments of his life, his wife is of no use.

TWENTY-TWO

As long as Mejda and the others were around, Malloban had to put up at the mess with various distastes and discomforts of mind and body.

Seven months went by this way. Then Mejda went away. But even back home, Malloban no longer found the environment particularly favorable. No medicine or diet seems able to put any flesh on Monu's bones; the way she's deteriorating day after day—thinking of it, sometimes he has to forget the puzzle of domestic life, that its nectar is poisonous fruit, or not poisonous but with thorns, like boinchi fruit; that boinchi fruit—is not or is a poisonous fruit; more than love and fear, pity seems again to be a far greater thing.

A man named Amaresh—middle-class, or maybe somewhat higher class—was coming to see Utpala all the time these days. Amaresh can't be called fair-complexioned—but he's got style in his long frame, and even though the superiority of his mind is not as striking as the brilliance of his body, when it comes to worldly wisdom, he's adroit and proficient—almost at the level of accomplishment. He's around thirty-five or thirty-six. He's been married for

eight or ten years—he has three kids. When and where he
met Utpala—it could be that they're meeting for the first
time here and now, Malloban knows nothing. Amaresh
and Utpala spend a lot of time playing music and singing
together—whether or not their meetings are decent and
normal is a question that occupies Malloban's mind much
of the time, in the office and at home—he forgets about
Monu—that thing called pity seems very insignificant.
In this way, the days went by. These days Monu sleeps
downstairs with Malloban. Amaresh comes riding his
bicycle. He leaves the bicycle downstairs and goes upstairs;
he leaves at nine, nine-thirty, ten at night. Then Malloban
goes upstairs to eat. There, he sees Utpala so lost in her
own thoughts that he's afraid to interrupt her by talking. As
Malloban eats, he thinks that among all the people Utpala
knows, this Amaresh is a creature apart: where everyone
else has fumbled, resorted to tricks, Amaresh has put his
hand right on the main plug, like an expert mechanic.

As he thinks, the grains of rice in his plate look to him
like dirty, stiffened, dried-out flattened rice; he'll have to
eat this flattened rice like fragments of brick with dal, with
fish stew; everything's mixed together like brick dust, but
still, in fear of something or other—fear of whom, why,
he can't quite put his finger on it, he—slowly chewing,
he sends it all down through his silent throat. But still,
Malloban doesn't find the courage to ask his wife a single
thing about Amaresh.

He's understood, even if his own mind is Swati's dew-
pearl, his body is not nacre, but a slimy thing like a snail or
a shellfish. That in all the folds of this body, there is meat—
lumps of meat, Malloban has become aware. As if the body

were a strange goiter—his mind is hanging from the edge of a pinch of time for a couple of days within creation.

Monu is eating; but halfway through her food she has put her head down on the table and fallen asleep. Malloban wondered whether he should wake Monu, or would Utpala take Monu by the ear and wake her from the lie of sleep into the stuffy untruth of the world of this room?

Monu is sleeping, no one's paying attention to her.

As if an incomparable chitrini has now become a shankhini—sitting at one end of the table—Utpala's not eating anything; a china dish is sitting in front of her, but there's no rice in it, she could have turned her eyes towards quite a bit of open world beyond the terrace, but she's turned her back to the terrace and is staring at the wall—but still her gaze has gone very far—the wall in between is no obstacle—her eyes are not hurting—there's no illumination in them either—there is, like a light source you can make out from the light's reflection, like the coming and going of all that, a kind of cold silent thoughtfulness; Malloban has never seen Utpala so still in such a strange frame of mind. Is this good or bad?

What does this mean?

"Aren't you going to eat anything, Utpala?" Malloban said, clearing his throat. "Aren't you going to eat?" This time he had to say it a bit louder.

Stirring slightly, Utpala corrected her sitting posture. How had she been sitting? That pose is not quite appropriate for this moment. A few hours ago, it would have been fine to sit this way; but now this sort of posture isn't good enough. Besides, her sari has somehow come loose around her waist—very loose—it's come completely undone—as

soon as Utpala stands up the whole sari will slip off and
make a heap on the ground.

"What time of night is it?"

"It's late, at least ten o'clock," said Malloban.

"We're eating late tonight."

"No, it's not all that late, I wasn't hungry."

"A winter night—ten isn't early."

"Who were you talking with? For so long? Who?"
Quietly posing one question after another, Malloban paused
for an answer.

"Oh, someone." Utpala put her hands to her waist and
straightened her sari.

It's not that Malloban hadn't seen it; drawing in a
bit of the night's cold, he looked again; Utpala saw that
Malloban saw; Malloban's not a sharp observer, his wife
knows that, but still as she tightened the cloth around her
waist it seemed to Utpala: the man's more than a little sly,
he's got his eye on me; but what have I done, I haven't
done anything.

"That he's someone, even I could see—"

"So what then—you've seen him."

"Yes, when he was going upstairs, I saw the man. He
left his bicycle downstairs."

"Then?"

"I don't know him, you know. I've never seen him in
this house before." Utpala sprinkled a little water on her
dish, spread it out with her hand, put a couple spoonfuls of
rice on top and said, "The people who come to see me, do
you know all of them?"

"More or less, I recognize them."

"Who comes, let's hear it."

"I can't tell you their names, but if I saw them in the street I wouldn't be mistaken."

"I take it you know them all by sight—"

"That's right." Turning to the central point, Malloban said, "But who is this?"

Mixing a little butter with the rice and rubbing in a little salt and green chili, Utpala said, "With what aim do they come here?"

"How would I know? That's a matter for your own personal communication. I've never gone sticking my nose into that."

Utpala was carefully picking the seeds out of the chili, she said, "Good for you, but why are you sticking your nose in today?"

"Monu's fallen asleep."

"I can see that."

"Should I wake her?"

"Not now."

"This rice is like flattened rice."

"It's gone cold, that's why it seems stiff."

"Why does Thakur do the cooking and leave so far ahead of time?"

"These winter nights—how long do you expect him to sit around? He wants to finish whatever he has to do and go home—all the way to Chetla—" This time, as she spoke, Utpala started eating; there are still a few chili seeds in the rice; she's picked out most of them.

"Of course, I don't keep him sitting here."

"I didn't say you were responsible—"

Malloban thought, the grating quality is gone from Utpala's words, she's speaking naturally, her voice is gentle, even if affection is not intended in the conversation, there's a grasp of inner significance, there's a sense of grammaticality—for Malloban's convenience.

Amaresh came again the next evening. Amaresh left his bicycle locked up in a corner of Malloban's room. Malloban had come home from the office and lain down on the bed. Turning to cast a look at him, Amaresh said, "What are you doing?"

"Lying here."

"You came from the office?"

"I just came."

"Is your wife home?"

"Yes, Utpala's upstairs."

Amaresh went upstairs. Malloban put out the light. But a light from outside is filtering into the room, making Amaresh's bicycle glitter. Whenever Malloban gets to thinking this and that—he goes into the darkness; cutting through the darkness like a fine blade, the bicycle blazes up again; Malloban thought, this is the fight of the subconscious and the conscious, the unconscious draws him to sleep—to death; consciousness tells him to stay alert, to mould and arrange; fine, he'll mould and arrange.

He hasn't had tea, has he? Should he have some? The cook had come and asked if babu would have tea and snacks or not—Malloban had said no to him.

Should he go to Goldighi? No, he's not going anywhere. Malloban kept lying there. Upstairs a few songs have been sung. The esraj has been played for a while too. Songs come easily—the way the last leaf of the winter comes out on the branches of shimul, jarul, and piyal—in the boy's voice; he can sing very naturally, very well; in some places the boy's personality shows through with wonderful clarity (why is he calling Amaresh 'the boy'? Since he still has a bit of the vigor of morning clinging to his frame?)—is that just vocal skill? Sincerity? Soul? Malloban can't tell. Of course, he's heard better singing than Amaresh's, but this too hits hard—even if in two ways—as if the night jasmine of artistry still strikes deepest. Was it Utpala playing the esraj? Then, for the past hour or hour and a half, everything has been quiet—there doesn't seem to be anyone there. That bicycle is glittering and glimmering all too much; and its owner is gleaming up there like a scaly snake after milk? Malloban feels like unlocking the bicycle, taking it down into the street, spinning the pedals, and speeding off—the way its owner, even when he's lost all sense of direction, nevertheless at the start of the evening ends up right at house number thirty-two—the way a shadow, running after a body all day without catching it, nevertheless in the dark of night merges with it inseparably—in this same way that Amaresh comes; in this same way, to some thirty-two, thirty-two hundred, thirty-two thousand—into the endless horizon, Malloban will go, will he?

Not going into the thirty-two-hundred-endless horizons, in the end he went out to Goldighi; when he came back, it was close to nine-thirty—he came and saw Amaresh's bicycle still leaning against the wall.

"Babu, should I bring your rice?"

"Why?"

"Ma said to bring it."

"Fine," Malloban said to the cook.

He ate the rice and paced for a long time inside his own room, but the bicycle didn't go anywhere.

Monu's sleeping on one side of the bed. Malloban looks at his watch, it's almost eleven; upstairs, the music starts up abrubtly a couple of times, for a few minutes at a time, as it descends into unfathomable silence.

Malloban lit a cheroot and sat down on the bed. Dong, the clock next door struck eleven. Maybe this time the boy will come down and go away. But he didn't come down. Malloban thought maybe the music would start up again. But that didn't happen either. As long as the singing, sarod-playing, laughing and joking was going on, he could throw stones in the dark and still keep himself busy. But everything's stopped now—too late at night, too dark, too cold: now what? What's happening now? Whatever's happening is happening: no use getting beaten by the riddles of his own mind. He made himself lighten up; at the thought of the fun going on upstairs, he started laughing; the bicycle looked like Amaresh's Nepali boy, the bicycle's glittering like the gleaming of a kukri; as if, sticking a kukri in his belt, Amaresh's Nepali servant were sitting there like an old heap in the total cold of the late night. If his master doesn't come down, there's no saving him, there's nothing; but still, he's an astonishing symbol, this Nepali, this stupid Nepali kukri—of today's world. The relationship between a woman and a man, between a human and a human, between a human and nature, has lost its subtlety—its success, its simplicity; it's lost its savor; in today's undiscriminating world, severing all the neat bonds of relationship, the immeasurable strength of mind of innumerable utter fools have cleared themselves a path like a stupid Nepali kukri. Then how can time nature god (if there is any such person) be thought of today? As lord?

As friend? As wife? No, not that. Not like a husband, wife, or friend; endeavors will be undertaken as a Nepali kukri; Malloban can't sleep.

It's not Malloban's fault; it's not sleep's fault either; it's the fault of this world, of this century; but still, when he woke up at three in the morning, that meant he had fallen asleep at some point.

The bicycle's gone.

The cold is blowing in through the open door to the road. Malloban got up and closed the door.

TWENTY-THREE

The next day, when he came back in the evening from an outing, Malloban heard from the cook that Amaresh Babu had gone into the mistress's room.

Malloban ate dinner, read the newspaper, smoked a cheroot; then he thought a few things; as he thought, he kept thinking thoughts for two or three hours.

At midnight, Amaresh came downstairs.

"You're still awake, Chandmohan Babu—" Calling out suddenly to Malloban, Amaresh pulled him out of his numb state under the covers. Malloban's name is not Chandmohan. Amaresh just wants to wag his tongue and knock him flat with the name, calling Malloban by that name. Fine. Malloban pulled the blanket off his face and said, "I was falling asleep."

"And then?" Amaresh said, opening the bicycle lock.

"Where are you going?"

"Ahiritola."

"At this hour?"

"I have to go down into the Ganga at Ahiritola."

"At this hour?"

"I'm going swimming."

This time Malloban said nothing more. Propping his backbone against the pillow, he sat up a bit.

"That's kind of a club of ours. A bunch of guys splash down on all fours like sacks of salt to swim at Ahiritola, in the Ganga."

Wondering why Amaresh said "munish (farmhands)" and not "manush (people)," Malloban said, "They'll be bathing in the Ganga at this hour?"

"Not bathing, mister. We weren't born to mark our foreheads with the clay of the Ganga, brother. Swimming— to see who can go how far, who can get ahead of whom—"

"Oh," Malloban said.

The boy put down the bicycle and sat down on the edge of Malloban's table.

"Sit in a chair."

"I'm fine here. Will you come see us swim, Chandmohan Babu?"

"Now? At this hour?"

"All right, fine. You're an old man, so you can come for the Baruni bathing festival, it'll be warm then."

Malloban said, "But will people really be swimming at Ahiritola Ghat tonight?"

"What have I just been telling you. Even the girls will come to see it—" lifting the stiff-polished New Cut shoe on his right foot, Amaresh said, "I touch this blessed cowhide and swear that gentlemen's daughters will all flock to see our games; prostitutes will go, all the prostitutes in all the neighborhoods over that way—"

Malloban lit a cheroot.

"There won't be any scuffle between the whores and the well-bred girls, sir, no one will drive anyone away. Even these women will admit unequivocally that those women are human too, sir."

Malloban was thinking, taken aback: is this that same Amaresh? With this man, Utpala stays up until midnight! The kind of man who, even if he doesn't spit as he talks, builds up spit on his tongue and teeth—not actually, of course, metaphorically speaking—this boy is just that vapid, unintelligent, exuberant sort of man, with a long frame; a good build; a handsome face; and for all that, this chaff is a gem for Utpala. That's how it is. Creation is a statistitian, but it's not an accountant—what fatal mistakes have been somehow mixed like poison into the blood of the universe, into the flow of its unbroken design!

"But it's not enough to admit it," Malloban said. "You'll have to show them how to become human."

"That's a big social problem——"

Malloban said, puffing on a cheroot, "Everything is everything. Sure, what kind of societal riddle can you solve by going to see someone swimming? But yes, what you said, quite a bit of brotherly love—sisterly love—brotherhood—but they've got very bad diseases."

"Sure, they do, but girls can't give diseases to other girls. They mingle with great sincerity, but women are not men after all——"

Malloban took the cheroot out of his mouth and, for a little while, with the eyes of his skin and the eyes of his mind, with all four eyes, looked steadily at Amaresh, and then he said, "There are plenty of boys there too."

"Very few of them are totally shameless."

At that, Malloban twisted his neck; straightening his neck, taking a drag on his cheroot, twisting his neck again, he looked once at Amaresh. But he didn't say what he thought he was going to say, he said something pointless, "Won't they get pneumonia swimming in such cold."

"Sure—they'll get over it. Or they'll die."

"What are you saying? Why should they die! So, how did you get to know my wife?" Malloban said, shifting natures from cat to cheetah, from cheetah to cat.

"I'm going now, Malloban Babu, it's late."

Malloban noticed his cheroot had gone out. Striking a match and lighting the cheroot, Malloban suddenly sprang up like a big baby jackal and said, "You brought the bicycle here and went straight upstairs. When and where did you get to know my wife, won't you tell me?"

Malloban has asked a very straightforward question, which had a straightforward answer; it wasn't that Amaresh couldn't answer now in a natural way, but still he said, "I'll come again to your place, after all. Maybe I'll tell you another time." Amaresh took a tin of cigarettes out of his overcoat pocket. Lighting a cigarette, he said, "What you were saying about societal problems? Nothing much can be done about that if there isn't economic growth in all our lives. That's the place to start. Of course, we can't be blind to societal issues either."

Malloban said, flattening Amaresh's words like an old dirty newspaper under his own feelings and understanding, "You're quite well off yourself—"

"Your wife is doing fine too. I can see that." Amaresh didn't seem to be hinting at anything with that; he laughed in an affectionate, innocent way, as if he hadn't made any kind of sly hint at all. But the laugh went by, Amaresh's face took on a different expression; pursuing clarity through obscurity, Malloban still didn't find a trace of it, he remained staring at the blazing ember of his cheroot. The room had gone silent. Only the smoke from one man's cheroot and the other's cigarette were talking across each other.

"Looking at me, would you think my current wife is the third, Malloban Babu?"

Amaresh said, "The first wife is still alive, she lives at her father's house, I'm not going to live with her. Number two, Katyayani, is dead. This is number three. This wife has three kids. There's another one coming in the month of Magh."

Malloban sensed that from Amaresh's tone of voice, the build of his body, the whole of his inner self—some firm, (but) facile self-content is oozing out. Today's partisans of lust, and what's not quite lust but still perverse—in this world of values in disorder, what Amaresh is saying is quite natural; natural, therefore good? Good or bad? And he himself? Malloban was staring at a few ash-laden sparks from his cheroot, thinking. Disordered values? The disorderly think that this is order. What are orderly values? What is this in Malloban's opinion? If he himself wants orderly values, then why are they so patently absent from his own house?

"It's getting late."

"It's twelve o'clock." Amaresh said.

"Twelve o'clock on a winter night . . . What did you want from my wife?"

"If you go on talking, it's bound to get late—"

"I can see that. I haven't seen you there before?"

Shaking his head along with the cigarette smoke he exhaled, with the smoke spinning, Amaresh said, "I didn't know you all were here."

"How did you find out, then?"

"Chandmohan-da, sugar doesn't smell ants. The ants have to go and find it themselves," Amaresh said, feeling jovial. "You people want to live all swept clean, or at least without touching anything unclean, but it doesn't work like that; ants and sugar are reduced to specks of dust; have you ever seen sugar picking out the ants and eating them?"

Malloban was thinking: there's no heat in Amaresh's words; as if instead of two legs, Amaresh had eight, like a spider, he keeps nattering on all the time; since he's been seeing sometimes deep-green, sometimes deep-red female spiders—all his life. He's got a slick look; he's been spoiled by money—by quite a few girls. Is Utpala fueling the fire too?

Malloban took the cheroot from his mouth and was trying to guess how far the fuel had gone—what kind—

He somehow thought himself into a deeply meditative state; he said out loud, "Sit down, sit down, Amaresh Babu, sit down." But for a long time now, his mind had stopped the movement of his tongue; it had been momentarily slain; his cheroot had gone out—

"I'm going, Malloban Babu."

"All right—"

"I'll come tomorrow."

"Do come. Do come."

TWENTY-FOUR

About seven days later, not long before ten, after Amaresh had left, Malloban went upstairs for dinner.

When he got upstairs, he saw that Utpala was sitting inert on one side of the dinner table; Monu was sleeping with her head on the table.

"We eat dinner so late these days," Malloban said.

"What time is it?"

"Ten."

"Is ten all that late?"

"Not for everyone," said Malloban. "Monu's fallen asleep without eating. Maybe not because it's late, maybe because the cold is too much for her."

Utpala said, "You could eat dinner earlier if you wanted. The kitchen is right by your room. Monu could eat with you too—"

"Yes, tomorrow we'll have to start doing things differently. That man who comes to see you all the time these days, he's the reason things have gotten a little chaotic in this house. Who is he?"

"I don't know him."

"What do you mean?"

"I mean—" Utpala wasn't in the mood for banalities, she said, "I don't know him. That's what it means. It means—take this and chew on it, that's what it means. Eh Monu! Monu!" Utpala called out suddenly.

"Don't wake her, let her be—don't wake her up."

"Won't she eat?"

"No."

"Every day now, she falls asleep without eating."

"If you wake her up now, she won't eat anything, she won't let us eat anything either." Malloban took Monu in his arms and carried her off to bed.

When he came back, Utpala had wiped off the table with a towel and was setting out two china dishes, drinking glasses, salt, lime, and green chilies in a big saucer. She had on a handloom sari of a texture like a parul flower, as if sprung from nature itself—with a broad red border. She looked incomparably beautiful, like some Sita, Sarama, Draupadi, or Chitraseni, more thoroughly content than she could have hoped.

"Come on—come and eat—" Utpala said.

Malloban sat down in a chair and said, "When did Amaresh come?"

"In the evening."

"Even before I came back from the office?"

"I don't know when you come back."

"Yes, when I came back from the office, I saw his bicycle in my room."

"He comes by bicycle, does he?" Utpala said. "I didn't know."

"Tonight, he left before ten! One time I noticed he didn't budge until eleven or twelve at night. Who is he?"

"I don't know him."

Utpala put seven luchi or so on Malloban's plate and took three for herself. There were bowls of fried eggplant, chholar dal, and potatoes. There was a saucepan of milk—it's gone cold. Everything's gone limp, the luchis are stiff; no one feels hungry, but still, breaking off a piece of this, taking a nibble of that, a pinch of something else, negligently, reluctantly, they had to keep eating—stopping now and then as they ate to exchange a few words.

"You don't know him—then how does he get into your room?"

"Is this my house?"

Malloban said, "That's the impression I've been under all this time. Now with Amaresh coming and going, you've decided to foist ownership on me and call me to account for his activities?"

Utpala had eaten one half luchi out of the three by now; unable to decide what to do with the other two and a half, for the time being she folded her hands and said, looking at Malloban, "Whether it's my house or your house, it's right over your nose that Amaresh is finding his way into my room every day. What have you done about it? What are you going to do?"

Malloban had finished two luchi, some chholar dal, and one slice of fried eggplant. Taking a sip from his water glass, wetting his lips and tongue and chilling his teeth, he said, "I didn't know you didn't know him."

"What did you think?"

"You don't know him?"

"I told you I don't know him."

"He's not someone from your father's family?"

"No."

"Did he go to college with you?"

"I went to a girls' college—up to second year. Your mind is straying."

"He's nobody—you never saw him before now?" Malloban said, dumbfounded. "So?"

"What do you mean, so?" Frowning, Utpala looked at Malloban.

"So, it seems you're opening up to him more and more every day." Malloban looked at Utpala with gentle-stern eyes; communicating some demand and yet withdrawing it, he kept looking with motionless, tireless eyes for a while. He said, "Ever since he came, you have such a coy, charming look—one I've hardly ever seen before. The way you talk, the way you act—did that garden bloom at the touch of wedding water once? Is it getting cloud water now? All the better, it seems."

Utpala had been putting it off until now, finally she started eating. Her lips hardly moved, or not at all, a smile blossomed and vanished at once from her face, a smile of amusement—of pain—maybe of some unconscious spasm of the facial muscles—

Utpala had eaten half a luchi, she was eating the other half.

"It's been about fifteen days since Amaresh started coming to see me. He spends four, five, six hours here, the light stays on in my room; the light even stays off for a long time; sometimes we think maybe you're coming up; if you did come up, you'd make a scene—" Finishing off the last piece of luchi, Utpala said, "Whether you would or not I don't know, but a man is a man, he can't go without

trouble; there would have been a scene by this time;
Amaresh wouldn't have kept quiet either."

"Why, what goes on up there?"

"Why should I tell you?"

"So, I'm supposed to go ask that stranger, that boy?"

"What do you mean, couldn't you come up and see for
yourself? It's been fifteen days. You've seen the man rushing
upstairs every one of those days. He's even sat downstairs
and talked with you a few times. What did you think of
Amaresh, after talking to him?"

Malloban didn't try to eat any more. Lighting a cigarette
with his food-soiled hand, he said, "You didn't eat your
luchi—"

"I'm not hungry."

"Will Amaresh come tomorrow?"

"That he will," Utpala broke off another piece of luchi,
rousing herself in a courageous effort to arouse her hunger,
and said, "Can you forbid him to come to this house again?"

Utpala stood up.

"What happened?"

"I'm sleepy."

"Sit down, sit down, I have something to say to you—"

"No, no, I can't sit any longer. Every joint of both my
legs is hurting. Say what you have to say, I'm standing here
listening—"

Malloban didn't bother to smoke his cigarette. Dropping
it into his water glass, he said, "What are you going to do
about Amaresh? Tell me."

Utpala put her own water glass to her lips and sipped
a little water, then rinsed her mouth with the rest and spat
it out onto the terrace. On the table, in a little saucer,

there were a few paan. Putting two paan in her mouth and looking with agitation—gradually graced with calm, then with a kind of still compassion, at Malloban, she said, laughing, "There's nothing to be done."

"What are you saying!" Malloban said, as if beating a bird's wings on Utpala's vision. "Do you realize what you're saying?"

"I'm saying what I'm saying," said Utpala, staring at Malloban with those same satiated eyes, without faltering. "Why don't you come up tomorrow and set things right—?"

Malloban lowered his eyes from Utpala's face and began, far more with the harsh heat of the light cast by his eyes than by his mind, to fill the whole room; slowly light came into his mind; he saw the light had gone cold; Malloban was thinking: he could never set things right himself; to climb over a wall in the dark of night and steal fruit even from his own tree, or to beat up the one who stole it, wasn't his temperament; good or bad, he had a strange sort of temperament; he had no inclination to send his friends after them; it would all become public, the little domestic peace he did have would shatter into a million pieces. But won't Utpala help him?

Malloban dumped out the water in his glass, poured himself a little water from the metal pot, and gulped it down—washed his face and hands. It felt good, as if a little Christ-like peace had been established on earth, but still, Malloban had no desire to leap over the horse of logic to eat the grass of solace; he thought it over: his suspicion about Utpala and Amaresh's relationship, as a husband now past forty—today's world being what it is, it's not that he can't have such a suspicion about his lovely twenty-eight-year-old shankhini wife. But Utpala is not that kind of woman at all, it's not right to mistrust her. Amaresh comes every day, it's true; he stays for a few hours, but they're like sister and brother; at most they banter, like a younger brother-in-law and his sister-in-law, nothing more than that—surrounding Malloban's unbroken analysis of life's good and evil, the blue vitriol of the blue-gray smoke of Macropolo cigarettes plunged Malloban deep in blissful meditation, in an astonishing lack of concern, he didn't feel the need to think anything anymore.

"Amaresh has a lot of money?"

"No. He doesn't have much."

"Still, he's better off than we are?"

Utpala said in an incoherent, disembodied way, "I can't say. It could be."

"He looks like an aristocrat's son."

Utpala had been standing on the other side of the table; she'd come to this side, at some point she'd gone over there again; she was standing the whole time, not sitting, she said, "Oh, you're only thinking of money and pedigree. I don't get worked up about all that. They used to have a lot of land, now there are a lot of shareholders. The estate is falling apart—now they don't have much of anything—"

"How old is Amaresh?"

"He must be thirty-six or thirty-seven—"

"What's his wife like?"

"Like any old-time landowner's wife—" Utpala said in a calm cool expressionless way, as if she were reporting information, nothing more, and still a drop or two of her blood cells conferred on herself, her words, the cold night air all around, a kind of beyond-reporting.

"He's not old-time—he's from our time—"

"Yes, he himself thinks that he's from the future." With a sluggish laugh, trembling with a little muscle-spasm, stricken with mistrust, or with a disarmed, sincere smile as if indulging a child, Utpala said, "He's got plenty of brains in his head. But his family is holding him back. He's got three kids; he'll have another one in Magh."

"You've found out that much," said Malloban, as if confronted with a buffalo's tail waving in the darkness like a cobra.

Utpala picked up a paan from the saucer of paan and put it down again distractedly. There were some spices in the saucer. Stirring them around with her finger, she picked up a clove. Biting at the clove with her teeth, she said, "Amaresh comes to see me every day. He stays with me into the night. He tells me everything. Why wouldn't I find out that much?"

On the verge of baring his teeth like a cheetah, Malloban said like a scavenger crow, with tired, troubled eyes, "Does he tell you everything himself—do everything himself? It's you who's making him talk. He stays here until twelve or one in the morning—because you're here, you're letting him stay. You're not going to set this straight?"

"There's no way to set it straight."

"No way?"

"No way. Don't complain."

Utpala gave Malloban a piercing, unblinking look, she looked at him with such affection—with such a depth of compassion!—Malloban was looking at Utpala's eyes—he looked and looked until he couldn't look any more.

"Listen."

Malloban turned and looked at Utpala's eyes again. But he just kept on looking. Utpala too kept on standing there, holding Malloban's eyes with her own. It felt so good to both of them. But this is an otherworldly wifely intimacy—beyond the river of life—maybe it will happen one day—maybe it won't.

"Tell me."

"I've told you already," said Utpala.

"An untouchable like Amaresh—"

"What do you mean untouchable? He's a Brahmin boy—"

"Will that whore still come to see you?"

"You've got a foul mouth," Utpala said, emitting heat like a turned-off oven where there's no fire and still, in the ashes, a pervasive burning. In the winter night, Malloban didn't mind the heat. Standing there radiating heat, gathering fire from some unknown other cavity, Utpala said, "He only stays until ten or eleven. Now it's two. Now the winter night has set in—"

"Set in?" Looking at Utpala's desirous, compliant body, Malloban steadied himself a bit and said, "When does a winter night set in?"

"At just this time—"

"But this time won't be here for all time, all this will break up tomorrow at dawn."

"It won't be dawn anymore."

"How can you say that?"

Malloban stood up. Burrowing his feet into his slippers and pulling his shawl tightly around him, as he ran his eyes all over the room's darkness, he saw that Utpala had come to stand even closer to him.

The two of them went and lay down on the bed. Utpala said to Malloban, "It won't be dawn anymore, we won't have to know. See how cold the winter night is, the cold night of a pair of geese in a bed of hay, how marvelous it is, really, even better since it's long. Really, it will never be over anymore."

Malloban felt astonished. That he will never have to wake up again, winter, best of all, in this disorderly degenerate time in society, a bed at night, finest of all, this same winter night will nevermore end, Utpala will be pressed against Malloban's time for all time in the infinite winter season. It seemed a moment of unprecedented beauty. And yet how can it be? There's no history? It's disintegrated, let Utpala go away, taking Malloban with her? There's time, isn't there? There's no time? Utpala has severed herself and gone away, with him, from all of time? Deep, deep, this winter night. Inexpressible—when not from a river but from within hard dry rubies and emeralds, there is water flowing; with that water-goddess, to lie still in this winter night.

The night will never end?

No.

Our night will never end, Utpala?

It won't. It won't.

The winter night will never run out?

No.

They'll never run out, the cold, the night, our sleep?

No, no, they won't run out.

They'll never run out, the cold, the night, our sleep?

They won't run out. They won't run out.

They'll never run out, the cold, the night, our sleep?

No, no, they won't run out.

They'll never run out, the cold, the night, our sleep?
They won't run out. They won't run out. Never—

Talking himself into a frenzy, this light and darkness,
sun, falcons, big winds, the eight divine female powers, the
prostitutes, the roar of Utpala's laughter, the sound of the
sea, the sound of blood, the sound of death, the rumor of
the never-ending flow of the winter night, listening to all
this, Malloban came awake. He had been sleeping with his
head on the table. He looked and saw the room dark; all
the plates and dishes had been removed from the table and
the scraps cleared away, he had not noticed; the table was
neat and clean—glittering like the back of a black reptile.
Malloban couldn't figure out when he had fallen asleep.
Just a moment ago, he was seeing Utpala, he had lain down
on the bed, he was listening to her speak—all this he had
seen in sleep, heard from the throat of the unknowable
otherworld? Then up to what point had he heard in a
waking state. Malloban bent his head and tried, in the dark,
to understand . . .

He remembered. He felt morose. So, since nothing
would ever change, since he'd never manage to do
anything, Utpala had let him fall asleep on the dirty table;
she cleared the table; she put up the mosquito net; she got
in bed and even fell asleep—but didn't she even think she
should wake Malloban?

ACKNOWLEDGMENTS

I want to thank my agent Kanishka Gupta and my editors—Ananya Bhatia for taking on this translation and Rea Mukherjee for seeing it through, as well as the whole team at Penguin India; thanks to the designers for respecting my wish to have a bird on the cover.

Bhalobasha to A., for everything.

Hugs to bondhus Sumita and Pooja for their encouragement in the early stages.

Anek dhonnobad to Protima di and Prasenjit da of AIIS Kolkata for reading the original with me when I was an advanced language student in 2011.

Many thanks to my academic advisers George Hart, Raka Ray, Sylvia Tiwon, and Michael Mascuch for supporting my research on Jibanananda, and to Chana Kronfeld for her translation studies courses and advising on my MA thesis.

Dhonnobad to Sridhar Sarkar, whose copy of *Malloban* ended up in my hands, and to Arunabha Sarkar for encouragement and clarifications.

Nandri to Kannan M. and the whole Pondi family for their confidence in my potential as a translator and their warm support over the years.

Hugs to my family for all their support.

And to Kuheli and Ariktam, this bit is for you: "From the direction of the morning fog, they went flying far off in the other direction to draw out the very earth, those crows, to bring out the shining sun for everyone—even those who aren't crows, aren't birds . . ."